The Life of a
Colonial Fugitive

By Jonathan E. Lee:
Revolutionary Patriot, War Criminal, Hero of
the Kingdom of Siam.

CHAPTER 1:
A Warrior's Reminiscence

June 1783: The blazing-orange, tropical sun creeps above the rattan-studded horizon to announce the dawn of another sweltering day in the island paradise of Phuket, Siam. The gentle ocean breeze wafts the smell of decaying flesh into my nares as I survey the carnage of the past days' fight from behind a thick palm. Less than a yard away, the dark skin of a dying enemy soldier is covered with vicious red ants, slowly eating him alive as he bellows out in pain-laden death throes. I climb out from my jungle concealment and walk across the sandy beach to ask the dying man in the Siamese tongue if he would like for me to speed the end of his life. The dying soldier is too feeble for speech, barely managing a slight affirmative nod of head. I unsheathe my sword and run the man thru his heart, stepping back respectfully as the blood gushes from the jagged wound that I have inflicted upon his chest. As I watch the life drain from the young man's sad face, I find myself reminiscing on the first time I gazed into a pair of youthful eyes prematurely aged by the horrors of war.

September 1778: An otherwise dull Tuesday suddenly transformed itself into a frenzy of excitement as my older brother, Henry Lee III, arrived unexpectedly in Leesylvania[1] for the first time since the beginning of the colonial revolution. Mother and I had been taking our tea under the shade of our estate's great wrap-around porch while observing our slaves working

---

1. "Leesylvania": The unofficial name of the region of Northern Virginia that lies adjacent to the Potomac River, near the present site of Washington City, where the Lee Family settled after emigrating from the British Isles.

the adjacent cotton fields when Henry's silhouette had appeared over the horizon. Mother jumped up excitedly, spilling her tea and leaving a stain on the white-washed railing, which she quite uncharacteristically ignored as she cantered down the steps to meet him.

I waved half-heartedly at my brother but remained seated for we had not parted on favorable terms and I was, frankly, not excited by the prospect of his return. Henry clambered down from his raggedly-thin appearing horse, gave Mother a hug, and then walked towards me with an obvious limp in his right leg. I shall never forget the look of my brother's gaze that day; gone was the shine of boyish innocence from his icy-blue eyes, replaced now with the penetrating stare of a man who had witnessed the animalistic brutality of combat. Henry's body was transformed too, skinny now, his two-year-old uniform that had been so painstakingly sown by my mother years ago hanging from his bones like beggar's rags. Quite ashamed of my initial indifference, I rose from my rocking chair and hurried to assist Henry as he clumsily scaled our porch stairs.

"This leg of mine, it's never been the same since my horse fell atop me at Brandywine Creek. Anytime I ride for more n' an hour it cramps up somethin' awful." Henry mumbled as his face twisted into a grimace of agony.

"Where are you ridin' in from, General Washington's camp at West Point?" I inquired, eager to make conversation to disguise the expression of shock that was plastered about my face, shock at the haggardness of my brother's appearance.

"Yes and a fine improvement from last season's accommodations at Valley Forge, that's for sure. Many a good patriot froze to death in

that snowy hell." Henry muttered bitterly.
"Enough with all this talk on the damned war,
let us speak on somethin' more pleasant. How
are the plans for your grand tour of Europe
progressin', Jonathan?"

"Tell us about this General Washington, Henry!
Is he the hero the papers make him out to be?"
Mother loudly interjected to Henry's great
annoyance.

 "I asked a polite and simple question about my
brother, mama!" Henry shouted, his voice hard
and calloused. "Why all this subterfuge?"

"The trip's cancelled; it's too dangerous to
cross the Atlantic anyhow now that France has
entered the war." I stated matter-of-factly as
I pulled my shoulders back and puffed out my
chest. I've decided to join the Continental
Army; I leave in three days to join my
regiment."

 "And Father has given his consent for this
tomfoolery!" Henry demanded, his voice filled
with bitter disdain.

"Father has his reservations, the same
reservations he had when you were commissioned,
as I recall."

"I didn't realize I was kin to such a fool,
throwin' away an opportunity to travel and
study in Europe with full expenses
paid no less! Don't you see my gimp leg, boy,
and how ragged I look cause of this endless
fight. Are you really that blind or are you
just plain stupid!" Henry exclaimed, his tone
condescending and full of rage.

"Let us speak no more on this!" Mother begged
as she fought back heartbroken tears.

"Speakin' isn't what I had in mind for him!" I blared across the patio, loud enough to distract the field slaves in the distance, my fists gripped white-knuckled in anger.

"I said enough!" Scolded Mother as if we were both still young boys rather than fully grown men. "This is my home and y'all will respect it!"

My brother and I glared at one another, our eyes full of hatred, fists tightly clinched. Mother moved between us, and with the greatest reluctance, for hot tempers run thick in my family's blood, Henry and I both backed down, unclenched our fists and entering my mother's home, giving one another a wide berth as we dusted off our boots and stepped through the doorway. The three of us found Father reading the local news pamphlet in his trusty, old hickory rocking chair, oblivious to the commotion that we had caused outside due to an affliction with pronounced deafness due to his time spent fighting in the French and Indian War. Henry strolled over to him and they embraced warmly, a broad toothless and somewhat unnatural smile shone across my father's old, wrinkled, perpetually frowning face. I stormed off to my room, ignoring Father's thunderous calls behind me as I slammed the door shut and then fixated my gaze out of my bedroom window, lost in my thoughts. Later that evening, the family gathered for a grand feast, prepared by our house servants in my brother's honor, a feast that I begrudgingly attended after incessant nagging by Mother.

"Mother tells me you've just returned from Georgia, Father. How do you find our brethren in the Deep South are holdin' up amidst all this chaos?" Henry inquired between generously-sized and eagerly partaken bites of roasted pheasant.

"They're holdin' up better than we are, that's for certain, though I expect the British will try to change that soon enough. The British generals have no choice but to take the war to the south, as important a port as Charleston has become now and is becoming more so every day. Find yourself any new musket in the hands of a continental and I can guarantee you that it was smuggled in through Charleston or Savannah on a blockade runner. Yes, the British will strike in the Deep South before this time next year, mark my words." Father stated as he peered over his reading spectacles, his news pamphlet lying in its customary location, unfolded open upon his lap.

"And what of the cotton trade, Pa? Rumor has it that the Georgians are growin' strains that produce twice, even thrice, the usual bounty." Henry asked as he shook his head in disgust.

"Indeed they are, and growin' it in the fertile soils of the Mississippi territories in flagrant violation of their treaty with the Cherokee. They float the cotton down the river to Mobile and New Orleans where the British blockade remains porous; the cost of shippin' by barge down the rivers is less than what we pay to travel our cotton by wagon over less than an eighth of the distance." Father said dryly with a wizened look of despair creeping across his brow. "I fear Leesylvania may only be suitable for growin' soybeans and vegetables in the years to come. It is a thought that I have been losin' much sleep over since my return, almost as much sleep as I have been losin' worryin' on you, Henry. Now, tell us of the Revolution; in what shape is the Continental Army to be found presently? It's hard to find information in the pamphlets these days that is worth the paper it's printed on."

"The war's not a subject for the ears of women and children, Pa." Said Henry coldly, staring in my eyes and as he articulated the word 'children,' making it clear to all present whom he was referring to.

My brother and I spoke little over the next three days, save for common courtesies that were uttered without eye contact and in guttural tones. When Henry saddled his horse to return to his regiment at West Point, I could not find it in my heart to bid him farewell. I watched enviously as my brother's war mount lazily meandered down our plantation's dusty central path, little knowing that it might well be the last time I laid eyes upon my brother in this life. This was knowledge that would have pleased me at the time, for in my youth I could not have imagined how much I would long for the company of my family, my brother included, in the dark years to come.

CHAPTER 2:
The 11th Virginian Continental Regiment

October 1778: I reported for duty at the command tent of the 11th Virginian Continental Regiment on the First of October, a fine breezy autumn day, ideal for the training mission on which our newly constituted regiment was preparing to embark. I found the 11th Virginia's commanding officer, Colonel Woodrow, pacing around his expansive, luxuriously furnished, command tent in an aggressive agitation. Colonel Woodrow hardly acknowledged my presence as I begged permission to enter the command tent, responding only with a casually lukewarm wave of his hand in the general direction of an uncomfortable appearing wicker chair, the only unpadded item of furniture amongst the dozen over-stuffed chairs and couches that were littered about the massive tent's periphery, the center of the command tent being occupied by a solid oak table, its surface covered with topographic maps. I took a seat in the wicker chair, twiddling my thumbs and feeling quite out of place as I watched my new commander pace to-and-fro, gesticulating wildly with his saber and muttering to himself unintelligibly. Colonel Woodrow was a lean, muscular officer with a frame more befitting a twenty-year old enlisted man than a forty-year old regimental commander. His uniform fit smartly and his saber shone brightly in the sunlight that flooded through the tents open folds, his saber shining nearly as brightly as the Colonel's impeccably polished leather boots, boots of fine European craftsmanship, probably Neapolitan I thought as I gazed about the room, my mind eager for any distraction from my sweaty-palmed anxiety as I sat waiting. The minutes ticked by, unbearable minutes that felt like hours, until suddenly the Colonel ceased his roaming soliloquy and squared his body directly in front of mine, his powerful jaw tightly clinched.

"Do you know how many white families have been killed by the Injun this year, Mr. Lee?" Colonel Woodrow shouted as he leaned in towards me, his body inches from my paling face.

"No Sir, but any number is surely too many, Sir."

"But you don't know how many are dead, do you, you haven't the least clue!" The Colonel rasped in condescending exasperation.

"N-n-no Sir, I confess my regrettable ignorance." I stuttered as I spoke, my eyes downtrodden, nervous sweat filling my boots.

"Ignorant or apathetic, Mr. Lee; either way, you are not alone. The fact of the matter is that nobody knows, not even myself, because no one is bothered enough by the deaths of those hardworking Christians to keep track of how many the redskins are slaying with their blood-stained tomahawks, skinning their women and children like ranchers harvesting rawhide! I was raised on the frontier and I watched my entire family butchered by the savages before I had reached my seventh birthday. I saved my wretched skin by hiding under a pile of cow dung, covered in shit like a damn coward deserves. God how I burnt for revenge, from the depths of my blackened soul I burned, hating myself as much as I hated the savages. But that pathetic boy grew into a man, Mr. Lee, a man who knows the God-given truth that revenge is not only man's greatest pleasure but also his greatest duty!"

I stared at the Colonel, unable to speak, standing stiff at attention, my eyes staring straight ahead, not daring to move a muscle, the perspiration dripping down my pantaloons into my tight fitting, now sweat drenched, unbroken boots that had been busily rubbing blisters onto my virgin feet all day, blisters that now burned with fierce intensity as my salty sweat seeped into the vesicles. I wiggled my aching toes as the Colonel continued his pressured tirade, my commander seemingly now oblivious again to my presence, speaking only to himself and to the god that he both worshipped and despised.

"Cobleskill and Wyoming Valley, these are just the latest sites of the heathen massacres; mass killings instigated, supplied, and financed by the godforsaken British. I intend to avenge these atrocities by returning the favor upon their wicked perpetrators tenfold, with God as my witness!" My frightful new commandant gazed skyward as he shouted his fiery pledge, shaking his fist at the heavens.

Colonel Woodrow stalked across his command tent to a map that hung from the far wall, motioning for me to follow after him. The Colonel's map ranged from Canada to Virginia, from the Atlantic coast to the unspoiled nether regions of Kentucke, containing a level topographic detail found only on military maps of the highest quality.

"Our official orders arrived a week ago, signed by the great General Washington himself. The mission will not be an easy one; the regiment will lose as much blood as it draws." Colonel Woodrow quietly mumbled, the raging tempest that had been storming inside him beginning to calm. "Our God-given task is to mold this soft, pathetic rabble of clueless farm boys into a functional Continental regiment before the end of the month…"

"That only leaves two weeks, Sir, barely enough time to train the men to march and to shoot!" I feebly protested.

"Barely enough time, indeed." The Colonel retorted, a wizened professorial tone creeping into his stone-bitter voice. "Nonetheless, that is our task at hand for our departure date is nonnegotiable. On October the First, we will begin our march from Virginia to the frontiers of Western New York where we will serve to guard the white settlements from the predations of the soulless redskins. Our secondary objective will be to scout the wilderness, providing reconnaissance to thwart surprise attacks on General Washington's rear from British Canada. I need not remind you that just last year General Burgoyne marched a force of six thousand British regulars through this very same territory." The Colonel stated matter-of-factly, his face contorted with an incongruous mixture of cautious reserve and brazen enthusiasm.

I stood speechless for the tales of the horrors of frontier warfare were well known to all Virginians. Visions of scalping, raping, and pillaging of innocent civilians rampaged through my mind as the Colonel gesticulated towards his war map in vivid exuberance. Later that afternoon, Colonel Woodrow gathered the other Virginian gentlemen who were assigned to our regiment into his command tent and officially commissioned us as officers of the Continental Army. After swearing our oaths of office on the Colonel's well-worn Bible, the new regimental cadre, myself included, received our command assignments and then we were abruptly dismissed to take charge of our units.

The 11th Virginian Continental Regiment stood at two hundred and fifty men strong, half the size of a regular infantry line regiment. Colonel Woodrow commanded the regiment with support from his executive officer, a newly commissioned Major purportedly selected for his military prowess but in reality chosen for his

social connections with members of the General
Assembly of Virginia, a worthless man who
served little purpose other than to relay the
Colonel's orders to the company commanders. The
regiment was divided into five companies of
approximately forty-five men each, companies
that were designated Alpha, Bravo, Charlie,
Delta, and Echo Companies with a smaller sixth
company, designated Headquarters Company, which
consisted of the regimental command and support
staff. Each company was commanded by a newly
commissioned captain, save for headquarters
company which was commanded directly by Colonel
Woodrow. The five infantry companies were
proportioned into two platoons of twenty men
apiece, each platoon commanded by a young
Lieutenant. The 11th Virginia Continental
Regiment was a light infantry unit, meaning
that the regiment was designed for frontier
warfare where rapid movement through difficult
terrain, rather than brute force, won the day.
To achieve this goal the regiment was devoid of
cumbersome heavy artillery, carrying only two
small cannon, and the soldiers were hand-picked
from the hardy mountain folk of the western
Appalachian frontier of Virginia, a land where
days without food were a common occurrence and
hunting with a musket was a skill learnt in
childhood.

I was assigned to command Bravo Company
and I found my company's First Sergeant
impatiently waiting for me in front of the
company formation, the men in neatly lined
ranks and standing in stiff positions-of-
attention. The First Sergeant was a tall, lean,
muscular man with a coarsely wrinkled sun-
hardened face and equally hardened eyes. The
First Sergeant saluted me smartly with a brisk,
"First Sergeant Miller reporting for duty,
Sir," then he suddenly turned about to bark at
a man who had been slouching in formation. I
returned my First Sergeant's salute and then
turned to face my men, my limbs trembling with

anxiety as I stood quietly hoping that my pathetic bout of nerves didn't show through the façade of confidence that I was desperately trying to project. I cleared my throat and began to speak in my loudest and deepest intonation.

"My fellow Virginians, you have all volunteered to stand where you now stand through no coercion, only guided by your love for our beleaguered home. For this selfless commitment I commend you and it is the greatest honor of my life that I have been chosen, along with your platoon leaders and First Sergeant Miller, to lead you wherever the great State of Virginia deems our services most vital. As you may know, we have been ordered to proceed to Western New York to protect the defenseless settlements of that virgin country from the savages' merciless aggression. In the course of our duties, we will simultaneously serve to guard the rear flank of General Washington's Continental Army, which is currently stationed at West Point, against surprise attack from British Canada. Our mission will not be an easy one. The savage is as clever as he is brutal and he has known the terrain where we will meet him since his infancy. Thus we must train with an intensity that is equal to our task. Time is not on our side for we are scheduled to depart in one fortnight and there will be no time for further drill once we have marched north. I will now turn over the formation to First Sergeant Miller; that is all." I excused myself from the formation having judged, correctly, that First Sergeant Miller would want time alone with the soldiers without my presence to distract them. I walked to a spot that was out of sight behind a nearby tent where I could listen to my First Sergeant as he spoke.

"Private Carpenter, why in fuck's name are you moving in my formation, Private Carpenter!" First Sergeant expelled in a guttural bellow.

I snuck a peak from around my hiding place and abhorrently witnessed First Sergeant Miller grabbing the frightened, young Private by his throat and choking him until the lad turned blue in his face and dropped onto his knees.

"You WILL address me as First Sergeant, you WILL obey my commands without question, or you WILL end up like this sorry heap of manure! Is that understood?"

First Sergeant Miller was answered only by silence, a silence that enraged him so that he lifted his musket and hit the nearest soldier squarely in the face with its butt, instantly knocking the young man unconscious. I stared aghast, willing myself to step forward to halt these atrocities but at the last moment decided to hold my tongue for I was new to the military and I had no illusions that the power of my commands rested solely in the hands of the First Sergeant who enforced them. Bravo Company was now clustered together into an unnaturally tight formation, like a herd of buffalo circling for protection from a hungry pack of wolves, the men standing shoulder-to-shoulder, shuddering in fear as every man's eyes focused straight forward, staring into the distance, not daring a glance in First Sergeant's direction. First Sergeant strutted through the ranks like a parading peacock, correcting each soldier one-by-one with terse commands such as, "feet at a forty five degree angle, hands along the seams of your pants, tuck in that damn pointy chin!" Unnerved and feeling emasculated, my self-confidence shredded into tatters, I retired to my tent for a shot of brandy and a nap, staring at the tent's breeze-fluttering ceiling as the last drops of liquor trickled their way down my lumpy throat.

The next two weeks were a flurry of
controlled chaos as First Sergeant Miller and I
drilled the soldiers in the military arts of
marching, marksmanship, and modern battle
tactics. I was pleasantly surprised to learn
that virtually all of my men were indeed
seasoned marksmen, an artifact of their less-
than-privileged upraising, childhoods spent
scavenging for food in the untamed mountains of
Appalachia. However, the men's background also
made them naturally independently-minded,
making discipline difficult to enforce. I
rapidly learnt to appreciate, though never to
fully condone, my First Sergeant's disciplinary
rigor as a necessary evil. Within two weeks'
time, First Sergeant Miller and I had
successfully transformed the men of Bravo
Company from a rabble of farm boys into an
orderly collection of lethal soldiers. The
initial discipline difficulties and the
occasional, surreptitious bouts of drunkenness
aside, by the end of the fortnight I was
confident in the ability of my Bravo Company to
face our soulless enemy in the heat of combat.
Indeed, even Colonel Woodrow had a rare look of
approval across his hate-chiseled face as he
reviewed our formation during his final
inspection before the regiment's deployment to
the New York frontier.

On the 22nd of September, I was awakened
by First Sergeant's booming voice and I
sleepily opened the drapes of my tent to find
him standing beside an individual with the most
off-putting appearance I had ever beholden.
First Sergeant's companion's name was
Wolfslayer, a red-skinned man of limited height
and slight build who nonetheless managed to
radiate an engulfing aura of intimidation about
his person. The vicious appearing tomahawk
tucked in the Indian's belt and his deer hide
clothes only added to the man's threatening
appearance and I thought to myself that I would
be loath to meet him in the woods alone at

night. First Sergeant Miller flashed a tobacco-stained, toothy grin as he introduced the native as an old friend while stating, "an' I don't call many men my friend, it ain't a word I toss out easy now." Hailing from the Finger Lakes Region of New York, Wolfslayer had been assigned by Colonel Woodrow to serve as Bravo Company's frontier guide. I introduced myself to the Indian and inquired as to the nature of the unusual necklace that was hanging from his neck. Wolfslayer informed me that it was made out of the ears of Mohawk, Seneca and Cayuga warriors that he, a proud member of the Oneida tribe, had killed in battle during the intertribal civil war that still raged between the former members of the Iroquois Confederacy[2]. I made a note to myself not to ask about any of the other unusual articles of clothing that he was sporting then I dismissed him to First Sergeant's care while heading back to my tent for a final night's sleep before our deployment.

I rose early on the morning of September the 23rd to supervise the breaking of our camp and I was pleased to find my men working with great zeal, tearing down their tents and burying the heaping piles of refuse that our regiment had managed to produce during our brief stay. After a roaming inspection of the campsite with his Executive Officer in tow, and finding himself satisfied that all was in order, at 0630 Colonel Woodrow called the regiment to attention and we began our orderly march towards the frontier fields of death, Wolfslayer and First Sergeant marching by my side in front of the rank-and-file of our Bravo Company.

2. The Iroquois Confederacy: The most civilized of the Indian intertribal governments in the colonies, hundreds of years old when it fell into a civil war between the tribes allied with the Colonials and those allied with the British Crown. Of the six tribes, only the Oneidas and the Tuscarora fought alongside the Colonials while the remaining four tribes (the Seneca, Cayuga, Onondagas, and the Mohawks) allied with King George III.

CHAPTER 3:
Marching to Destiny

Though I commanded a steed, I chose to march alongside my soldiers, an action which I hoped would earn me credibility among the rank-and-file. The regiment marched an average of twenty-five miles per day and our feet blistered dreadfully, the blisters subsequently bursting and leaving us hobbled in pain, our excoriated feet soaking our woolen socks through with blood that at times ran briskly enough to seep its way all of the way through, leaving bloody footprints in our wake. First Sergeant protested that I was a fool not to ride my horse but I trudged onward, knowing that my men were suffering as much as I. In spite of the pleadings from our suffering feet and aching muscles, and the groans from our empty stomachs, groans which were quieted only by stale black biscuits and a meager daily ration of greasy bacon, the men and I marched onward without complaint or protestation. The regiment cheered loudly as we marched past Philadelphia's sentries and as we spotted the revolutionary flag waving proudly above our capital city, a city which five months prior had been shackled under the yoke of British occupation by General Howe's Royal Army. This brief elation was short-lived for Colonel Woodrow drove the regiment forward like the master of a team of whipped oxen being driven ahead of a cast iron plough. Throughout the march many of the regiment's officers, and much to my disgust, took to the habit of riding ahead of the formation and dining at pubs in the passing towns. This behavior abruptly ended on the 2nd of November, when Colonel Woodrow steered the regimental marching column to the left off of the main road and marched the 11th Virginian Regiment into the icy-cold wilderness of Northern New York. Our regiment was now in Indian-territory and a palpable hyper vigilance filled the men's faces as we filed down the pine needle coated, and often hardly discernible, frontier trail.

November 1778: The mind-numbing boredom of our weary trek was suddenly interrupted when Captain Waters, the commander of Alpha Company, came galloping up beside me, breathing deeply, his face projecting a contorted mix of fear, hate, and horror.

"How far back is Headquarters Company, Jonathan?" My co-equal in rank and position inquired, his voice filled with worry.

"About a mile back, marchin' behind Charlie Company today." I reported, unnerved by the appearance of the usually quite jovial Captain Waters.

Since leaving the main roads, Colonel Woodrow had ordered the regiment's companies to separate themselves spatially in one-half mile intervals, the Colonel's aim being to prevent the entire regiment from being attacked simultaneously in the event of an Indian ambush whilst still keeping the companies close enough to reinforce one another.

"What's gotten your dander up so mighty today, Brandon?" I inquired of Captain Waters excitedly.

"It's the most hellacious sight I ever seen, Jonathan. About a mile an' a half down the road in the Cherry Valley settlement, forty dead, butchered…just butchered. Ride with me to find the Colonel, he must be informed of this immediately." The Alpha Company Commander yelled as he kicked hard and high to spur his horse into a quick gallop.

"First Sergeant, post!" I ordered, my deep command-voice booming through the air.

"Sir!" First Sergeant replied as he jogged in my direction.

"Take charge of the company and have them break the formation into squads with at least twenty-five yards of distance between them. We have report of Indian war parties in the area and an ambush is likely waitin' ahead. First Sergeant, Wolfslayer is to travel in the rear with fourth platoon for his protection; I want you to personally keep him by your side and I need not remind you that he is quite irreplaceable." I ordered as I waved over the private who was tending to my stallion.

"Yes Sir, understood Sir." First Sergeant replied as he rendered a crisp salute.

I leapt onto my horse's back and spurred him into a sprint in pursuit of Captain Waters. The two of us, Captain Waters and I, reached Headquarters Company in tandem where we found Colonel Woodrow vigilantly scanning the horizon from the back of his tall, muscular, sky-black warhorse, the vicious beast snorting and spraying profuse quantities of thick snot onto the ground, its large brown eyes looking eager for a fight.

"Sir, I have a troublin' report from Cherry Valley. The entire settlement is…was slaughtered by the redskins; not a scalp remainin' on any man, woman or child, Sir." Captain Waters reported as he fought back tears from his eyes.

"Goddamn them, goddamn them all to hell!" The Colonel bellowed as he threw his arms around wildly, unsheathing his saber, its pristine blade gleaming brilliantly in the low November sun. "Go on Captain Waters, out with the rest of the details of this atrocity."

"My scouting party reported hearin' gunfire in the distance so I double-timed my company to the Cherry Valley settlement, Sir." Captain Waters stammered, his eyes meekly downcast, full of self-doubt. "The Indians had already done their deed and we arrived just as they were beginnin' to light fire to the cabins. My men chased them off, but only after sustainin' two casualties: one soldier from first platoon shot dead by musket fire and another from fourth platoon mortally wounded by a tomahawk that caught him square in the face as the Injun' he was chasin' ran away. We managed to drive them off and save most of the cabins and I left my company with orders to guard the village's perimeter and then rushed back to the rear to deliver this report. I thought you'd want to know immediately, Sir!"

Colonel Woodrow's face flushed red with rage as he stood in his saddle, waving his saber in a great circle and then pointing it into Captain Waters' face, so closely that it nearly touched the Alpha Company commander's face.

"You have abandoned your men in the heat of battle, Captain Waters, and God knows that I would be right to relieve you of command, which I may yet do after the battle is decided!" Colonel Woodrow growled. The Colonel looked down at the ground, his hands gripping his saber with paled knuckles, his horse's reins held so tightly that the poor animal reared its head back gasping for air. The Colonel stared at the ground, staring, staring, staring for a small eternity then pausing to breathe deeply before looking upwards, his expression now somewhat more relaxed, the burning of his enraged eyes now replaced with a rationally icy hatred. "Nonetheless, your company has performed adequately today and I commend you for it. We will establish our base camp at the Cherry Valley settlement. Captain Waters, your

Alpha Company will secure the village and defend-in-place until the rest of the regiment arrives. Captain Lee, your Bravo Company will pursue those red-skinned devils and bring me their scalps! Is my order understood, Captain Lee?"

"Scalps, Sir?" I whispered, as a twinge of scruples shot down my spine, my skin dimpling with fright-chilled goose bumps.

"The Lord curse you, yes, I said scalps goddam you!" The Colonel barked. "You will pursue the enemy, you will kill them to the last man, and then you will bring me their godforsaken bleeding scalps which I will have shipped to their crying squaws to let these barbarians know that the vengeance of the Christian God has finally arrived in this cursed land!"

My heart's reluctance shone through the thin façade of bravado that I desperately attempted to project. Not fooled in the least, reading my body language as if it were etched in script, the Colonel shot me a look of contempt not befitting of a street beggar or a brothel whore. The Colonel spat at the ground then looked down again as he attempted to regain his composure, a visible shudder of demonic rage traveling down his corpus. Seconds turned into minutes, yet the Colonel refused to look at me. Finally, the powerful man looked up, the anger once again faded from his face, now replaced by an expression of gentle fatherly wisdom.

"When you look at the victim's butchered carcasses you will appreciate my orders, Captain Lee. Captain Waters, none of the settler's bodies will be buried until the entire regiment has arrived to witness the scene of this crime. We must use this tragedy as an opportunity to educate our young soldiers as to the realities of the frontier, the realities of the Indian beast." The Colonel lectured in a calm, professorial tone. "Captain Waters, Captain Lee, take charge of your companies. Captain Frankton, post!"

"Yes, Sir!" Captain Frankton, the regimental personnel accountability officer responded as he trotted over to join our horseback conference.

"Inform the commanders of Charlie and Delta Companies to march their men towards the Cherry Valley settlement with all possible speed."

I hopped into my saddle and spurred my horse, riding off to take charge of Bravo Company, pained thoughts spinning through my mind like phantoms in a wicked ballet: thoughts of duty, thoughts of doubt, but most of all, thoughts of letting down my comrades, the soldiers whom divine providence had entrusted me to command. I arrived to find Bravo Company advancing towards Cherry Valley with textbook-quality speed, order, and caution. I complimented First Sergeant on the company's performance for I was well aware that he had been drilling the men every evening, late into the night, a routine that had been exceedingly unpopular with the rank-and-file, soldiers exhausted from the day's march whose only desire was the comfort of their dirty sleeping blanket. I gathered my company's platoon leaders about me and explained the Colonel's orders, comforted to see the uncertainty that I was feeling echoed on their faces. I began explaining my battle plan, a plan conceived on horseback as I had galloped back to my company at full speed. I ordered First Platoon to take the point position at the front of the company column, the most dangerous position in the marching formation for it is prone to ambush especially in the narrow topography of the wilderness trail on which we traveled, with its thick, overhanging pine forests on either side, the perfect concealment for Iroquois warriors. I must have given a decent call-to-arms for our meeting concluded with enthusiastic cries for revenge as I barked the orders for the men to form up and to commence the advance after our elusive foe.

Bravo Company proceeded forward towards the settlement as a cold, light drizzle sprinkled down upon our heads, just enough rain to bring out the stench of our flea-and-lice ridden wool uniforms and to make the forests crackle with the sounds of droplets rolling off pine needles, sounds that made our hyper-vigilant body hairs stand on end. One half mile from the settlement, the road narrowed and the putrid smell of rotting flesh began to burn through our nares, a harbinger of the tragedy that we were rapidly approaching. A mere hundred yards outside of the village, First Platoon suddenly halted and I spurred my horse to a quick trot to lay my eyes upon the distraction. I found it lying on the ground at Lieutenant Barnes' feet, a doll-like princess, not more than seven or eight years of age, with an angelic face that was blood-streaked and matted in what remained of her golden blond hair, her cranium covered in thick coagulated blood and covered with hungry black flies, the edges of the remnants of her scalp left jagged from the tomahawk slice that had ripped away her young life. Her clothes were missing and I dared not inspect closer to see if the poor child had been molested for my stomach was already churning with an eager vomitus that I willed myself to hold down, digging deep within to find the fortitude to drive my men onwards. Lieutenant Barnes and I made eye contact, a brief glance of mutual empathy, and sensing my unease, Lieutenant Barnes ordered the men to continue onwards. As we neared the settlement, I dismounted my steed and despite First Sergeant's colorful protestations, I traveled

at the front of the formation with Lieutenant
Barnes and the advance squad of First Platoon.

"Halt!" A Virginian voice rang out from the
tree line causing me to jump and then stand
petrified in the middle of the road, looking
quite the fool, whilst Lieutenant Barnes and
the soldiers of First Platoon immediately
dropped into a kneeling firing position.

"Sorry, Sir, but I was told to guard this road
an' me an' the boys is awful skittish 'cause of
the Indians that's about. We heard some war tom
toms not too long ago an', well, I'd be lyin'
if I told you we wasn't a little bit scared."
Stated the scruffy-faced private, an Alpha
Company soldier who looked far too short-in-
tooth to be carrying a musket.

"No need for apologies, Son. However, for your
peace of mind, do be aware that Colonel Woodrow
has ordered that the entire regiment is to
proceed to Cherry Valley along this route." I
stated professionally as I regained my wits.
"You can expect them from the south shortly.
Now, please direct us to the settlement, time
is not on our side this cursed day."

"The main village's a few hundred yards
straight ahead that-a-way over yonder, Sir. The
woods clear out real nice just a bit down the
road an' it is open field after that for a
ways." The private reported as he stood at
attention.

   The Cherry Valley settlement consisted of
seven solidly built, family-sized log cabins
arranged into two tidy rows that lay on either
side of the settlement's central rock and dirt
path. The burning remains of what had been a
large communal barn stood fifty yards from the
main village and the stench of the burning
flesh of its unfortunate equine inhabitants
mixed with the aroma of human decay as Bravo

Company marched past, every man struggling to occupy his mind with thoughts of something, anything, else. It occurred to me that the settlers must have grown accustomed to their many years of peaceful relations with their Indian neighbors for the appearance of the settlement's stockade, which had never been fully completed, spoke of a lackadaisical complacency. Indeed, the majority of the settlers appeared to have been slaughtered inside or about their cabins without any evident signs of resistance. Shaking my head in pity, I turned away from the melancholy scene and gathered my platoon leaders, First Sergeant, and Wolfslayer and then led them to speak with Captain Waters, who we found frantically directing Alpha Company's construction of a defensive perimeter.

"It's a less than ideal position for an encampment, with the tree line encroaching so closely to the western flank and hardly any cover save for half burnt cabins, wouldn't you agree, Captain Waters?" I inquired gently.

"Yes, but we're making do with the terrain that God has given us. My men are already at work on the trenches and I'm confident that we can hold off even an artillery supported attack if it were to come to that. Of course, were it my decision, I would prefer to hunt the redskins with you; damn the defense of this wretched graveyard." Captain Waters said through clinched teeth, not bothering to conceal his frustration.

Captain Waters noticed Wolfslayer's presence by my side and he shot him a penetratingly hateful stare, the captain clearly not pleased by the Indian's inclusion in our conversation. A prideful man, Wolfslayer defiantly puffed out his tattoo-covered chest and crossed his ink-laden arms as First Sergeant Miller interjected a harsh, "I've fought with this man for ten years and I'll damn well say that he's killed a hell of a lot more Indians than you have, Captain Waters, no disrespect intended, Sir!" Captain Waters' face flushed scarlet in embarrassed-anger and I swiftly interposed myself between the warring parties, fearing that they were about to come to blows.

"First Sergeant, have the men prepare themselves for a long march!" I commanded in my sternest tone. "Order them to bring provisions for three days and to leave the rest of the equipment under Alpha Company's watch. Bravo Company must travel lightly if we are to have any chance of catchin' the Indian war party. Wolfslayer, stand fast, your input on our course of pursuit is quite necessary for you know this country better than any other man present."

First Sergeant saluted, spun a picturesque about-face, and then marched off as I kneeled down and began drawing a rough depiction of the settlement at my feet in the muddy-pebbled soil.

"Which direction did the raidin' party flee, Captain Waters?" I asked loudly, making it clear that it was time to return to the business at hand and that I would not tolerate any more in-fighting.

"Due north, right into those woods over yonder, no more than three hours ago. The boys were eager to give pursuit but I was reticent to chase them into the forest with no reinforcements near at hand and with several of the settlers still clinging to life…perhaps it was an error of judgment." Captain Waters looked down, full of self-doubt, his voice cracking as he spoke. "The settlers, they all died not long after we arrived but I couldn't bring it to myself to leave them unguarded. One of them, a young girl who had been violated before they hacked her scalp off, she died in my arms Jonathan, not a hundred feet from where we stand."

I nodded as my mind cramped, searching for the right words, any words, words which cruelly eluded me as I was forced to settle instead for silence, staring at the ground, avoiding my colleague's tortured face. Captain Waters wiped his eyes with his dusty blood-covered sleeve as he regained his composure.

"Well, we did the best we could an' now there's a job to do." The Alpha Company commander stated as his posture straightened, the confidence returning to his prematurely aged eyes.

"And a fine job you did, Captain Waters. Now it's Bravo Company's turn to pick up this baton and to continue the mission. Wolfslayer, how do you recommend we begin our pursuit, you know this enemy far better than I."

"Is Mohawk, the enemy; maybe some Seneca too, but most is Mohawk. I am sure is Mohawk from tomahawk I sees' on ground, many tomahawk over there." My Indian guide pointed to the cabins as he spoke. "I think second, third, and fourth platoon should be march', making much noise when march', chasing behind Mohawk warrior on road. First platoon then travel fast, very quiet, in front of rest of Bravo Company. Mohawk will ambush Bravo Company on path and then first platoon attack from behind and kill them many! We surprise Mohawk and take many scalp!" Wolfslayer suggested as he licked his wickedly crooked, grinning lips like a wolf about to devour a tender lamb.

Though I was reluctant to divide my forces in this strange, foreboding land, and equally loath to allow an Indian to devise my battle plan, I quickly recognized that Wolfslayer's advice was sound and that I would be a fool not to take it.

"Very well, Wolfslayer and I will accompany first platoon while First Sergeant and Lieutenant Edwards lead the bulk of Bravo Company in a direct pursuit of the Mohawk via the forest path. Lieutenant Edwards, do you feel yourself prepared to command the main troop body?" I inquired, somewhat unsure of whether my young, inexperienced Lieutenant was equal to this important, and dangerous, assignment.

"It will be my greatest honor, Sir." The overly eager Lieutenant responded, his mouth salivating at the prospect of whetting his lips at the fountain of power.

"Then inform First Sergeant Miller that there has been a change of plans and that the company trains[3] will accompany the main troop-body. Lieutenant Barnes, order first platoon to discharge all unnecessary equipment onto the supply wagon, we embark in ten minutes." I ordered tersely as my men leapt into action.

3. Company Trains: The supply lines and equipment (wagons, etc.) of a military company.

CHAPTER 4
Innocence Lost

With First Platoon in tow, Wolfslayer set off at a frenzied pace into the evergreen forest. The forest was thick with closely packed slender pines, dense underbrush, and a carpet of pine needles that crunched under each footstep, making quiet movement difficult and compelling Wolfslayer to repeatedly turn back to admonish the platoon for making too much racket. The platoon traveled single file, myself in the center, our muskets held in the low-ready-position, our muzzles pointed to the ground with the musket stocks held firmly to our shoulders to allow for an immediate upwards pivot and firing should the enemy present himself. Moving in this irregular formation, I now understood why the Colonel had eschewed the standard blue, white, and red uniforms of the Continental Army, insisting instead that the men be clothed in brown frontiersman's garb, a manner of dress which had drawn incessant snickers from the bypassing formations of Continental Army Regulars during our march from Virginia but which now proved to be an exquisite camouflage against the green and brown foliage of the northern woodlands.

My spatial disorientation began the moment I entered the forest, causing me no small degree of uneasiness, an uneasiness soon alleviated by Wolfslayer's seemingly uncanny knowledge of the land. Wolfslayer led us without pause for twenty heart-pounding hours before suddenly stopping and declaring, much to my relief, that the day's march was completed. I ordered the men to eat a generous serving of rations, to hydrate their parched tongues with water from the nearby creek, and then to attempt sleep. Satisfied that the men were providing their weary bodies with adequate resuscitation, I willfully coaxed my cramping legs into walking over to Wolfslayer to discuss tomorrow's strategy.

"How will we know when to double back?" I asked Wolfslayer as we hungrily gnawed at our rations of stringy, venison jerky and rock-hard black biscuits.

"There one trail only, only one trail Mohawk and Seneca warrior know in this wood…trail that is narrow between, how you say…" Wolfslayer made an upward motion with his colorfully tattooed hands and arms into a triangular shape.

"Hills?" I suggested.

"Hmm, big hill." Said Wolfslayer, nodding his head in cautious agreement.

"Ah yes, you mean mountains." I replied, relieved that I had been able to decipher the Indian's speech, the Indian whose knowledge was so essential to my mission's success.

"Yes, two mountain come together and trail get small between mountain. Enemy ambush for Bravo Company is wait there. When ambush happen, we attack and…" Wolfslayer clapped his grimy hands together, hard, a sinister smile creeping across his dark face. "…then smash Mohawk from behind, they no will expect us and I will take many Mohawk scalp for my war belt!"

"How much farther is the remaining march?" I asked, my blistering, cracked feet praying that another twenty hour march didn't lie before them.

"Three, maybe four hour march. We stop here because white men very loud and snore when sleep. Mohawk there now, not far." Wolfslayer said through his rotten teeth. "Quietly move

tomorrow and wait for Bravo Company. You must
tell other white men, move like one with
forest. They make much, much noise today."

I lectured my half-asleep men on the
necessity of traveling with all possible
silence and then watched with amusement as
Wolfslayer forced himself to drink an
unnaturally copious amount of water before
lying on the damp ground for a short sleep, a
native trick for waking up early in the morning
during hunting excursions, the profuse
quantities of water compelling one to awaken to
urinate a few hours later. I lay on the muddy
ground, too tired to care as the cold and muddy
groundwater seeped into my clothes, covering my
face with my handkerchief in a feeble attempt
to protect my exposed skin from the hoard of
thirsty black flies and mosquitoes which were
buzzing about us in thick black clouds,
punishing my men and I with their unrivaled
tenacity. I closed my eyes and I was awoken far
too soon after by an energetic Wolfslayer, my
body still weary from yesterday's travels and
feeling as if I hadn't slept even a wink. I
reached up to feel my burning face and my hands
discovered several dozen large welts, courtesy
of the black flies, and I marveled at how tired
I must have been to sleep through such a
phlebotomy. Rising slowly from the ground, I
attempted to shake the caked mud off my
clothing and then I walked over to awaken the
rest of my platoon.

I commanded the men to eat a quick
breakfast and then to fill their canteens to
the brim at the creek, a creek which ran crisp
and cool as it wound its way through the virgin
forest. As difficult as yesterday's trek had
been, today's proved far worse as the woods
thickened to such a degree that it was
difficult to see for more than a yard in any
direction. The pine forest had transformed
itself into a deciduous mixture of glimmering

gold, orange, and red, a scene far more beautiful than any autumn tapestry in my beloved Virginia. Yet nature made us pay for this visual delight with an incorrigible cloud of biting insects that stalked us from the camp site leaving every soldier covered in raw welts about the face, scalp, and especially, at the waistbands, the area where our ammunition belts chaffed the bites with our every step, rubbing them raw until they bled with every motion. My men and I were all scratching our bites, cursing our lot in life, when Wolfslayer motioned for the platoon to freeze in place with a brisk upward hand signal. Ahead were deep Indian voices, voices speaking in a harsh native tongue, their words ringing menacingly through the forest.

"Too proud these Mohawk, they talk loud, think white men will only come on road where they watch for them. Drop musket, Captain, we go ahead to look; other white men need stay here and no talk. Very quiet must be!" Wolfslayer whispered directly into my ear.

Wolfslayer propped his musket against a tree and pulled out his feathered, razor-sharp tomahawk, advancing towards the enemy voices while I followed closely behind, my bayonet clasped tightly in my sweating palms. The ground rapidly ascended on a steep incline, transitioning into the base of a small rocky mount. The forest began to thin and Wolfslayer and I dropped to the ground, crawling forward silently on our bellies as the enemy voices grew louder. At the crest of the peak, we hid behind a large boulder and made visual contact with our foes. There were three dozen Mohawk warriors, an enemy that outnumbered my platoon of fifteen men by a ratio of more than two-to-one. The Mohawk appeared hard and war-crazed with tribal tattoos covering the skin that was exposed beneath their thick deer hide clothing, tomahawks at their sides, each warrior wearing his hair in a tall exotic hairstyle that stood straight on end pointing towards the sky and ran sagittally from front to the back down each man's otherwise shiny, hairless scalp, their faces cover with black-and-yellow war paint.

"Wait for Bravo Company arrive before attack them; Bravo Company be here soon." Said Wolfslayer, his voice hardly louder than the ambient rustle of the drying foliage that fluttered in the chill breeze as it clung tenaciously to the autumn trees that overhung our position.

"I concur, I will go back to gather my men." I stated as I silently stood, turning around while taking deliberate caution not to crunch the carpet of fallen leaves beneath my heavy boots.

"Bring quietly!" Wolfslayer rasped, still furious about the lack of noise discipline that my men had demonstrated during yesterday's march.

        I returned with fourteen of my soldiers, having left one man behind to guard the platoon's knapsacks. I positioned them in a crescent moon formation surrounding the mountain's apex, hidden behind the wood line yet still within line-of-sight of the Mohawk raiding party. Moments after we arrived, a panting Mohawk came running up the mountain from the forest below, sprinting past one of my men, who thankfully, was not spotted by the Mohawk, the Mohawk scout having been too preoccupied with shouting to his compatriots his warning in their heathen, native tongue to notice the threat that lay hidden directly in front of his eyes.

"This Mohawk say white men come on path below. Mohawk war chief now say 'tie the white women to trees,' Mohawk now go to fight Bravo Company on path below, they go now!" An excited Wolfslayer informed me as he withdrew a second tomahawk from his back-straps with his left hand to accompany the tomahawk that he already bore in his right.

"The white women? Did I hear you correctly, Wolfslayer?" I asked hurriedly.

"In woods, over there. Mohawk capture and make wives. Frenchman, name Scalpbuyer, he over there also. I see Scalpbuyer while you were get the platoon and make them ready for attack." Said Wolfslayer with a shrug of indifference.

I strained my eyes at the opposing wood line that lay at the far side of the mountain crest and I was amazed to behold two curly haired, blond women standing next to a youngish child with fiery red locks. Standing beside them was a cruel-looking white man, dressed in French fur trappers' attire, a musket resting against his side and a foot-long, curved bush-clearing knife clasped in his hand.

"We must attack now!" I exclaimed!

"Should wait, Bravo Company come soon. Mohawk have fool pride, yes, but he strong warrior still." Wolfslayer staunchly chastised.

Just then, musket fire rang out from the path below.

"Very smart, my friend First Sergeant. See Mohawk ambush and make Bravo Company attack first!" A grinning Wolfslayer exclaimed.

"The matter is decided for us! I will take five men to rescue the hostages while you, Lieutenant Barnes and the rest of the platoon engage the enemy in a frontal assault!" I commanded as I stood, ready for combat.

My soldiers were in position seconds
later, a finely tuned orchestra of death. We
rushed through the woods without a second to
lose for Wolfslayer would commence his assault
any moment. My squad of six circumscribed the
hilltop until we were one hundred and eighty
degrees from our starting point, now only yards
behind the captive women. Musket fire erupted
from Wolfslayer's position and was soon
followed by a bayonet charge into the Mohawk
encampment. The Mohawk's surprise was complete,
our assault a masterpiece of tactical artistry,
ten of the enemy dropping dead to the forest
floor before their remaining comrades had had
time to even find their weapons. Wolfslayer
charged into the fray, swinging his tomahawk
wildly, possessed with demonic furor as the men
of First Platoon enthusiastically followed
after him, their bayonets gleaming in the sun
and pointed straight at the terrified Mohawks.
I shouted, "now's our chance", and my small
group charged forward towards the captive
women. The women shrieked in horror as their
two Mohawk guards spun around to face us. I
raised my musket, close enough to the nearest
of the brawny Indian warriors to smell his
repugnant body odor, as I squeezed the trigger
and discharged a musket ball square into his
heavily muscled chest. The Mohawk brave was
lifted off his feet by the impact of my lead, a
look of surprise pasted on his contorted face,
a look that rapidly transfigured into a
horrible grimace of hate and fear as the blood
erupted from his mouth, accompanied by an
animalistic screech of death, the Mohawk's body
folding to the ground in a macabre, yet
dissonantly graceful, choreoform twist.

The fact that I had just taken a life
charged through my mind like an unbroken
stallion and I was surprised to feel a rush of
exhilaration and pride flowing through my body,
an emotion more powerful than any I had
experienced before either in love or in hate.

Witnessing the fate of his tribesman, the second Mohawk grabbed the redheaded child and rammed the barrel of his antique French musket between her scapulae while shrieking menacingly in his shrill native tongue, a sound not unlike that of a dying turkey being eaten by a fox. My body froze, my mind racing, unsure of how to react to such savagery. My indecisiveness was soon rectified by the private who was standing to my right, who raised his musket and put a round into the savage's shoulder, the shoulder exploding into an unrecognizable tangle of muscle, bone, and flesh. The Mohawk fired his weapon into his petrified hostage, blowing a shot into the unfortunate child's back that exited through her abdomen, leaving a great, gaping hole in its destructive wake whilst another of my soldiers administered the death blow to the howling Indian with a musket ball shot between his eagle-tattooed pectorals. The battle now winding down, I yelled to First Platoon to establish perimeter security while I glided towards the shaken women.

Now that I was upon them, I was surprised by how exceptionally young the surviving hostages were, the eldest girl perhaps sixteen years of age and the youngest no more than thirteen. Both bore bruises upon their petite faces and their dresses were ripped to tatters, tatters of cloth that fluttered in the cold wind, their exposed underclothes caked in coagulated blood. Taken aback by the women's wretched appearance, I stuttered as I asked them in the tenderest voice I could muster if they were injured. My inquiry was ignored as both women stood rigidly, seemingly oblivious to the carnage around them, staring into space with a gaze of a thousand yards.

"BOOM!"

Cannon shot rang out from the trail below as I stole a glance down from our precipice to see Bravo Company raining canister fire into the ill-fated Mohawk ambush party. The rout was completed as the men of Bravo Company surrounded the remaining Mohawk, Mohawk whose arms flapped wildly in the air in surrender, flapping like birds attempting to take flight. I looked behind me to see that Wolfslayer and Lieutenant Barnes boasted of a similar success: three Mohawk and the beaver-capped Frenchman held captive at musket point.

"Lieutenant Barnes, give me your status report! How many casualties have we suffered?" I demanded.

"One man dead and one dying from an abdominal wound, Sir!" My subordinate responded while professionally saluting me. "We count twenty-three Mohawk dead on the mountaintop and we have six captives in our possession—one is a French scalp trader who goes by the name of Scalpbuyer, Sir."

"Move our casualties, the rescued hostages, and the prisoners down the mountain to join the rest of the company. Leave one squad of men to sentry the heights to secure the road from surprise ambush while the rest of the company camps below for a respite." I ordered with a cracking voice as the shock of the battle, previously blunted by exhilaration, began to overcome me. "And Lieutenant, do be sure to have the deceased woman's body transported with us for a Christian burial with her people at the Cherry Valley settlement."

CHAPTER 5:
Mutiny in the Wilderness

I traveled down the mountain battlefield to the spindly, and thickly overgrown, trail where I gave a short oratory congratulating my soldiers for their battle performance. I instructed the men to sleep beside the road until dawn, a rest that they both needed and deserved. At daybreak we would embark on our triumphant return to the Cherry Valley settlement. I found myself a mostly dry patch of ground a few dozen yards from my men and under the frosty cold, star-filled New York sky a sound sleep soon overcame me. An hour before dawn, I was suddenly awakened to the sound of a man's screams echoing through the forest. I threw off my filthy field blanket and sprang to my feet, musket in hand, running towards the commotion and arriving seconds later to discover a sight that astounded my still-innocent eyes. Before me, I lay witness to First Sergeant Miller holding down a wallowing Mohawk with his crushing grip whilst Wolfslayer hacked the helpless savage's scalp off with three successive blows of his brightly feathered, ceremonial tomahawk.

"You there, halt!" I shouted as my body shook with an uncomfortable mix of fear and revulsion.

First Sergeant dropped the dying Indian and advanced towards me, taking broad, confident strides.

"You got no business in this, Sir. These here are Colonel's orders bein' carried out, bein' carried out right here, Sir!" First Sergeant bluntly stated as tobacco juices ran down his chin from the thick wad of Virginian-broadleaf that was tucked tightly in his upper cheek.

"This is my company and I am the rankin'
officer—not you, not your bloody savage, not
Colonel Woodrow, but me! You will cease and
desist or I shall have you hanged for
insubordination, so help me God!" I bellowed
with all of my air, praying that Lieutenant
Barnes and Lieutenant Edwards would be awakened
by the commotion for I was stricken with fear,
facing such barbarism alone in the wilderness.

    The words had hardly left my mouth when
First Sergeant ripped the musket from my
perspiring hands with a strength befitting a
plantation mule. I stood petrified in shock and
terror. A dark arm, an arm which I am now
certain belonged to Wolfslayer, reached around
my neck from behind me and must have choked me
into unconsciousness for when I arouse the noon
sun was bearing down upon me through the
dreary-gray autumn sky. Disoriented, I rose
from the ground to find myself alone and
unarmed—abandoned for dead in the wilderness.
My nose was broken and my face was caked in
dried blood. My head throbbed something awful
and I reached up and discovered a shallow
wound—a bullet trek from a pistol round that
had been fired at my forehead and had, by the
Grace of God or the Luck of the Devil, skirted
my skull and traveled circumferentially along
my skull bones, underneath my scalp, finally
exiting just above my neck. First Sergeant and
his Indian accomplice had shot me pointblank in
the head, an executioner's coup-de-grace,
leaving me for dead. But in their haste they
had not realized that their shot, though
bloody, hadn't proved fatal. Tears of despair
welled in my eyes but I refused them, burying
my despair and digging deep inside my soul for
the fortitude to regain my composure and to
press onward for I was stranded deep within
enemy territory and there was no time for self-
pity. I reached into my pantaloons and I was
relieved to feel the cold metal of my trusty

compass, a gift from my father that had been presented to me in silence the night I had departed my Leesylvania to begin my life as a soldier. I said a prayer of thanks and then began my dangerous, solitary trek back to the Cherry Valley settlement, the gift from my father guiding my way.

Despite my considerable anxiety, angst that was compounded by my yearning for revenge against Wolfslayer and my treacherous First Sergeant, I deliberately willed myself to tread slowly, silently picking my way through the pine forest, guided by my compass, fully cognizant that the path to Cherry Valley was guarded by roaming bands of Mohawk braves. My stomach churned with hunger and I gave thanks to The Lord when, midway to the settlement, He blessed me with a patch of delicious blueberries that lay directly adjacent to a sparkling autumn-chilled brook. I gobbled down the berries then eagerly whetted my parched tongue with the deliciously crisp water. I then washed the dried blood from my swollen face, blood which had run from my wound so thickly that it fell off in clumps into the stream. Feeling substantially better, I continued through the forest and arrived at the Cherry Valley settlement the next dawn, my white handkerchief knotted at the end of a fallen tree branch which I wove to-and-fro in the air so as not to become a casualty of the sentries that Colonel Woodrow had undoubtedly posted in sniping perches to guard the encampment.

"Halt, who goes there," demanded a hidden sentry.

"Captain Jonathan E. Lee, Bravo Company commander; show yourself!" I commanded, too tried for fear.

"Lord help me, what in damnation happened to you, Sir?" The sentry inquired with genuine concern.

"An ambush, Private, a treacherous, mutinous ambush. Take me to Colonel Woodrow immediately!"

Colonel Woodrow's command post was located in the center of the regimental encampment in a modestly-sized log cabin that had formerly functioned as the settlement's chapel. I found Colonel Woodrow seated behind a crucifix bearing desk that had once belonged to Cherry Valley's now deceased minister. I approached my commander and I offered him a salute but Colonel Woodrow refused look up from his papers to acknowledge me, instead continuing to ledger with his pheasant quill on a rolled parchment, seemingly oblivious to my presence.

"Sir, I have an urgent report, Sir!" I shouted so loudly that it frightened the Colonel, compelling him twitch violently, jumping in his seat, and forcing him to acknowledge me.

"An urgent report that can wait, Captain Lee!" The Colonel barked as he returned to his ledger. Disheartened, I stood stoically, my body rigidly held at the position-of-attention, standing in front of the Colonel's newly appropriated desk. My cautiously roving eyes noticed that the Colonel was dictating his parchment in invisible ink, a favorite tactic of General Washington's, whose love of the 'dark arts' of military subterfuge was as legendary among the Continental Army as his reputation for honesty was with the general population. After a good while, an agitated Colonel Woodrow put down his pen and handed his correspondence to a courier who immediately placed the parchment into a hidden compartment in his right boot heel.

"Corporal, deliver my message to General Washington at West Point with all possible speed. The rest of you will wait outside while I debrief Captain Lee."

As quickly as the words had left Colonel Woodrow's mouth, his command staff cleared out of the regimental headquarters like frightened rats escaping from a barn that had been lit ablaze. I heard the snap of the courier's whip cracking against his horse's flesh followed by the sound of the startled animal's hoof beats galloping away, bound for the Continental Army Headquarters at West Point.

"You look like a country beggar, Captain Lee, and your behavior is befitting of one." Colonel Woodrow growled, his face distorted into a sinister and condescending frown.

"But, Sir!" I protested.

"But, Sir! There are no 'but, Sirs' here, man! There is only an officer who has disobeyed the orders of his commander, disobeyed MY orders, and attempted to force HIS men to do the same! Look around you, you godforsaken coward! Smell the burnt flesh of the innocents, feel their rotting corpses if you must to get it through your damned wooden skull that we are fighting in a barbaric action against the Demons of Hell! You come here to report, Captain, then report on how your cowardice nearly let the murderers of these defenseless townspeople live to see another day, the murderers of these people whom we have sworn an oath before The Almighty God to protect from the heathens of Satan! Get out of my headquarters and drag your yellow tail back to your company, held between your legs like a disciplined pup!" The Colonel shouted. "Pray and repent to God Almighty for it is only by His grace that I do not relieve you of your command for this travesty!"

I exited the church and sulked across the Cherry Valley settlement, my head hung low in shame. I found Bravo Company camped on the far side of the village and I was greeted by First Sergeant Miller, a broad smile coursing over his wretched face as he welcomed me, welcomed me as if the events in the wilderness had never happened.

"Glad to see you well, Sir. The men are positioned to guard the village to the Northwest, that's our assigned sector, ya see. Colonel's ordered that we march back to Albany at daybreak." First Sergeant quipped joyfully as I stood shaking with rage, my soul pitch-black with murderous desire.

I forcefully commanded myself to restrain from acting on my impulse—to pull out my bayonet and ram it into my First Sergeant's throat. Oh how I wanted to slice that juicy neck wide open in a crescent deep enough to match his sarcastic grin! Breezing past First Sergeant Miller without either physical action or verbal reply, I made my way to the company command tent, catching a glimpse of Wolfslayer as he ducked into his tent as I passed. Wolfslayer was wearing a leather bandolier with a half-dozen scalps hanging from it, tied onto the belt by their hair. I noted that one of the scalps belonged to a white man, undoubtedly formerly the property of the Frenchman, known to the Indians as Scalpbuyer. I forced myself to ignore the Indian savage, painfully aware that any retribution on my part would find my neck in the hangman's noose before sunset.

I entered the Bravo Company command tent and officially took charge of my unit from Lieutenant Barnes, who had been acting as the company commander during my absence. Lieutenant Barnes gawked at my appearance with a befuddled look of fascination, remarking that he was told

by First Sergeant Miller that I had been
murdered during the night by a prowling Indian.
I waved my Lieutenant off, for I was in no mood
to talk, though I was silently grateful that at
least one person had not actively betrayed me.
Sleep did not find me in that long, lonely
night. Though my aching body begged for sleep
my troubled mind would not allow it as I sat
awake on my knapsack, training my loaded musket
on the flaps of my tent until the new day's sun
lazily crept over the horizon. Shortly after
dawn, the 11th Virginian Regiment began its
march towards Albany, setting the Cherry Valley
settlement ablaze as we departed lest its
spoils fall into Indian hands. The march to
Albany was long, cold, and silent.

CHAPTER 6
Treacherous Indictment

Thanksgiving Day 1778: My favorite boyhood holiday was transformed into a day that I relive in my tortured sleep every night that I manage to find the courage to will my weary eyes closed; it is the most potent of the rich tapestry of intrusive nightmares that torment my mind-and-body with a chronic insomnia that I would not wish upon my most hated enemy. It was a cold, snowy Thanksgiving Day, cold even by New York standards and absolutely frigid to a man accustomed to the temperate climate of fair Virginia. The rocky ground permeated our boots with a muddy slush as the 11th Virginian Regiment entered the brick and cobblestone city of Albany, New York. We were met by the raucous cheers of patriot sympathizers and by the equally enthusiastic jeers of British loyalists as we marched through the ideologically warring streets. Colonel Woodrow called the regiment to attention then dismissed the men for a three day furlough, a reward for our victory against our hated Mohawk foe. Colonel Woodrow ordered the regiment's cadre, myself included, to join him for dinner at the Arrowhead Inn, a local bar famous for its hardy cuisine and for its strong homebrewed drink. Loathing the thought of dining with First Sergeant Miller and Colonel Woodrow, I nonetheless obeyed my superior officer's command and gathered First Sergeant and my four platoon leaders about me, all of us changed from our frontier garb and into our boisterously ornamented dress uniforms, uniforms that were decorated with brightly shining brass buttons that stood in stark contrast to the darkness of our collective mood. My cadre and I walked through the breezy, snow-covered streets of Albany to the Arrowhead Inn in a frostily uncomfortable silence for I was still too filled with anger to utter a single word to any of them. The six of us walked through the heavy oak doors of the inn and found ourselves entering a large smoky room with row-after-row of long, dark maple wood tables, the walls adorned with the stuffed heads of enormous moose, broad-antlered elk, and handsome bucks. Mounted beneath each animal was the arrow with which it had been slain—the Inn's owner was half Indian and an avid bowman, a legendary hunter with a legendary reputation, a reputation that was known from the elk-and-moose populated forests of British Canada to the alligator-brimming swamps of the Georgia. I saw that the Arrowhead's owner was also a patriot for the Stars-and-Stripes of the revolutionary flag hung proudly on the wall behind the bar and the tables were clothed in similarly patriotic drapes.

Scanning the room as a thirsty deer scans a pond that is full alligators, I found Colonel Woodrow sitting at the head of a table located adjacent to the Inn's extreme right wall, the table directly beneath the head of a great brown bear, a bear the likes of which I had never seen with claws curved like daggers and a gaping mouth full of jagged teeth that surely could have ripped a man apart with one clasp of the its mighty jaws. Colonel Woodrow looked up slowly, acknowledging our presence with a crocodile smile.

Colonel Woodrow stood then bowed elegantly towards me. "Ah, our guests of honor have arrived. Take the seats at the head of our table, oh brave fighting men of Bravo Company! Captain Lee, I see you admiring the beast above me. The Innkeeper informs me that it is called a grizzly bear and was shot dead by the savages that live far west of the Mississippi River, savages who live even beyond the territories claimed by the cunt-licking French. Perhaps, when the war against the British has been decided in our favor, we can once again turn to

conquering the western lands that God has
willed to be ours!"

The stout New York ale flowed freely
around our table as the Colonel concluded his
speech. The cadre began to tear into the great
feast of freshly slain venison, glazed country
hare, and a hearty carrot-and-potato stew
whilst Colonel Woodrow loudly complimented
Bravo Company for our successful engagement
with the perpetrators of the Cherry Valley
massacre. I did my best to present an affront
of gratitude but my soul was torn at the
thought of the horrific crimes I had witnessed,
crimes that had been committed by men who were
ostensibly under my command. I tried to block
these images from my mind only to find them
immediately replaced by the memory of my
betrayal and near murder in the wilderness, the
sweat pouring down my brow and onto my fancy
white dress collar, the guilt-ridden terror
that was coursing through my body only
compounded more by the public castration of my
authority, an emasculation endorsed by the very
colonel who was now dining sloppily beside me
and raising toast-after-toast in my honor! I
avoided eye contact with Colonel Woodrow,
fearful that my gaze would reveal my utter
scorn for the man, a scorn that I knew I must
conceal lest I be sent home to Virginia in
shame or worse, find myself hanging from the
gallows. I fixated my gaze on the plate before
me and continued to pick at my food against the
loud protests of my bulging stomach for want of
something, anything, to occupy my racing mind.
I was staring down at this meal, staring down
lost in my thoughts when destiny burst through
the Arrowhead Inn's oak doors.

They entered the Arrowhead Inn with such
forceful speed that the slam of the doors set
the Inn's smoky air whirling like a waterspout.
Twenty in all, the armed posse wore the blue
woolen uniforms of Continental Army regulars

and bore shiny new French muskets, each soldier's weapon sporting an eighteen-inch bayonet. They flanked their commander, a Continental Army colonel, as he stormed over to our nervous table with his saber drawn, swinging it wildly in the air before planting it point down into our table, inches from Colonel Woodrow's panic-stricken face.

"Colonel Woodrow, I am Colonel Harrison of the 6th New York Regiment and you and your officers are under confinement"

"Under what fool's authority?" Colonel Woodrow demanded bitterly as he banged his fist against the table with such force that it knocked over several mugs of ale.

"You are charged with the murder of Felipe Gaston, the nephew of the Governor of New York, whose scalp your redskin attempted to sell to a merchant on Penny Street." Replied the powerfully built New York commander, his voice stone hard with confidence, his authority engulfing the room.

It was then that I noticed Wolfslayer, his hands bound, standing at the far side of the Arrowhead Inn and guarded at bayonet-point. Wolfslayer had a smug look of satisfaction on his face—odd, I thought, for a man accused of a hanging offense. Our hands now bound tightly in painful twine that cut into the flesh, Colonel Woodrow, First Sergeant, the rest of the cadre, and I were led down the dark roads that led out of Albany. We exited the cobblestone paved city streets and then we were led by our captors across frozen farm grounds to the 6th New York Regiment's field headquarters, a sprawling mass of thin cloth tents that reeked of sewage and spoiled meats, a smell that the brown rats that were darting from tent-to-tent evidently found quite irresistible. Upon arrival, we were formed into an uncomfortable line outside the regimental command tent where Colonel Harrison now sat interrogating Wolfslayer, the drapes of the tent pulled tightly shut. The sounds inside were muffled for the command tent, unlike the tents of the rank-and-file, was constructed of thick, double-layered deer hide. Nonetheless, barely a minute had passed before I heard Colonel Harrison's enraged roar blasting through the tent walls as he shouted to Wolfslayer, "If I discover that you do speak English, boy, I shall take pleasure in personally wrapping the noose around your goddamn neck! Private, remove this savage from my office and see that his arms and legs are triple bound with our thinnest rope until the bone is showing on his wrists!"

Wolfslayer was roughly manhandled from the command tent by a gruff-appearing soldier. A second musketman exited the command tent and approached Colonel Woodrow, motioning for him to march inside. An unbearable lull of silence followed Colonel Woodrow into the command tent, my ears straining in vain for any morsel of my commander's interrogation, a silence that was only interrupted by a Corporal appearing at the tent's entrance to beckon First Sergeant Miller inside for questioning. The sweat began to fall precipitously from my brow as I was struck by the revelation that Colonel Woodrow and First Sergeant might be passing the culpability for their war crimes onto my defenseless and lonely scalp. I tried to calm myself, thinking that no military officer would stoop to such peasant deception. It was a quaint hope, a hope that was rapidly demolished when Colonel Woodrow and First Sergeant Miller strolled from the command tent unbound, their faces bearing a vile look of satisfaction that they had borrowed from Satan himself.

I watched the two fiends canter past me in tandem as I yearned for my musket and cursed myself for not ending their godforsaken lives when I might have had the opportunity. I cringed pitifully as two of Colonel Harrison's soldiers shoved me into the command tent, both of the soldiers snickering as they made light comments about the noose that would soon stretch my neck. I was shoved in front of Colonel Harrison as one of my escorts, the broad-shouldered musketman to my right, buckled my legs with a swift stroke of his weapon into the crook of my knee, sending me crashing to the ground into a kneeling position. I looked at the New York commander, my eyes begging for empathy—indeed, it pains me to admit, I would have even accepted pity. Colonel Harrison's eyes hardened like iron poured into an ice-chilled mold, narrowing into snakelike slits, the sight of which ripped all hope for mercy out of my soul and dashed it onto the ground into broken pieces. It was at that dark moment, that endless pit of fiery hell that is forever etched into my most fearsome night tremors, that I decided that I would preserve my life no matter the cost to my honor, my family name, and the goddamn hollow oath that I swore alongside the traitors in my regiment before a God who will undoubtedly punish me in eternity for what I did.

Colonel Harrison began citing in a crisp staccato the war crimes of which I stood accused. I had scalped defenseless natives and ordered their scalps sold by my dimwitted Indian guide—both capital crimes in their own right. But worse, I had scalped the Frenchman, Scalpbuyer, a Frenchman who fate would have it was a distant blood relation of the powerful Governor of New York, a governor whose personal quest for vengeance was only exacerbated by my country's recently signed alliance with the Kingdom of France, a kingdom that would not take lightly the execution of one of its citizens by a Virginian. For these offenses, I was informed, I would be hanged at daybreak, no reason to delay lest the French discover my

crimes while I was still living and thus create
a diplomatic quagmire that Colonel Harrison
bluntly explained our nascent country could not
afford.

    Strangely, upon hearing the New York
commander's words, I was overcome by a wave of
calm that rippled down my tense perspiring
corpus, Colonel Harrison enunciating my death
sentence with a banker's monotone. My worst
fears had been realized, and like a wild hog
cornered by hunting hounds, I had nothing to
lose and everything to gain. As the New York
commander rambled on, reveling in the graphic
details of my imminent execution as his
soldiers shamelessly chuckled, I worked my
wrists loose from their painful bind, twisting
them so that my flesh rubbed off onto the sharp
hemp fibers, my fresh blood lubricating my
right hand free. I waited for another round of
laughter, joining in myself with a jolly laugh
as I lunged forward with the speed of a country
hare and slammed into the legs of my nearest
guard, grasping him behind his legs as I used
my body weight to force the stunned man hard
into the ground. I ripped my captor's musket
away then let loose a shot of lead into the
other guard, a man who was stood petrified with
a puzzled look on his face before he tumbled to
the ground with a great red spurt erupting from
the gaping exit wound that my shot had blown
into his back. I drove the musket's bayonet
into its former owner as the smile faded from
his face and was replaced by a toothily-crooked
death grimace. In one sweeping motion, I
retracted the bayonet from the guard's still
dying corpse and swung the musket in an arc
over my head, smashing the butt down onto
Colonel Harrison's cranium. I threw down the
musket and then leapt over Colonel Harrison's
desk, grabbing his pistol which I shoved then
against the disoriented man's temple with such
force that I drew blood.

I stormed from the command tent, hugging my hostage close to me lest one of his soldiers become emboldened enough to attempt a rescue shot. The men of the 6th New York Regiment were much distracted by their dinner rations and failed to notice us until Colonel Harrison let loose an ill-considered cry for help. I squeezed the trigger of my pistol and blew his skull apart then I dashed for one of the nearby cavalry stallions, which I leapt onto and then spurred it into a full sprint as the soldiers of the 6th New York Regiment stood paralyzed in disbelief at the scene that was unfolding before them. Fortune shined upon me for the stallion I had commandeered had the strength of an ox and the speed of a buck, clearing the wooden- barrel checkpoint that stood across the road that lead from the regiment's field camp in one smooth hurdle, my mount never failing to miss a stride as we sailed down the road into the wilderness before the New York sentries could fire off even a single volley. The regiment's officers attempted to pursue me on horseback but my lead was too great, my horse too swift, and I smiled as I watched my pursuers fade into the background, knowing that I had escaped.

I continued my solitary ride until well past midnight, making my way down the northbound roads until the roads ran out and transitioned into narrow, rocky trails, exhaustion finally catching up with me and I was compelled to stop for a brief sleep. I camped at a shallow lake, one of the thousands of lakes that the Good Lord had sparkled over the northern territories, blessing the colony's farmers with plentiful irrigation water for their vast fields of tall red, purple, orange, white, and yellow maize. I watered my steed and then retreated into the thick of the forest for a respite, soon overcome by the deep slumber of a man who has pushed his mind and body to their very limits. As my heavy eyelids fell shut, it

occurred to me that when I had awaken this
morning I had been a freeman and that the next
time I beheld the dawn sun it would be as a
fugitive.

    With morning came the most depressing
sunrise I have ever witnessed. I rummaged
through my stolen horse's saddlebag for
anything of value, rummaging like a plebeian
knave who has just stolen a lady's purse.
Inside it, I fortuitously discovered a civilian
change of clothes that were likely used by the
stallion's former owner during clandestine
forays into the steamy brothels of Albany, a
booming business in that city courtesy of the
frequent passage of Continental Army units from
West Point to Fort Ticonderoga and to the
various other outposts along the hotly
contested border with British Canada. My whore-
chasing comrade had also seen fit to conceal in
his saddlebag a spare pistol, a generous
complement of shot-and-powder, and a tomahawk
that was likely a war prize from skirmishes
with the Indians. My search completed, I bathed
in the lake and washed Colonel Harrison's blood
from my face and then changed into my newly
acquired civilian attire. I loaded the pistol
and tucked it into my waistband then I hung the
tomahawk, bag of powder, and sack of shot from
my belt. Fully dressed, I sat on a nearby tree
stump to ponder my plight.

    After much contemplation, I concluded
that travel by horse, though louder and thus
more dangerous than travel by foot due to the
threat from roaming Mohawk warriors and
marching units of Continentals, was my only
reasonable course of action for the mighty
northern winter was fast approaching, a winter
that would surely sap my life dry should I
remain in the wilderness to bear the brunt of
its fury. No, I would have to risk travel on
horseback, I decided, the only remaining
question was my destination. I was now a wanted

man and word of my crimes would rapidly
disseminate through the colonies like a plague
of the pox. No, establishing a new life in the
colonies was quite out of the question. But
what of Canada, I wondered? True, the war with
Britain would slow, and perhaps even halt the
news of my crimes from following me into the
royal protectorate, especially in the
francophone territories, lands with many
opportunities for a man of an agricultural
upbringing. Yet the war would not last forever
and the crimes I was accused of were far too
egregious to ever be forgotten. With the
signing of peace between the colonies and the
British Crown my life would again be in
jeopardy, even in the far reaches of Canada.
Nonetheless, I could discern no better option
so I rose from my wooden perch, entertained one
last gaze of the tranquilly glimmering lake,
and then mounted my stallion and rode off
towards French Canada at a measured pace.

CHAPTER 7
Escape from America

December 1779: I made my way northwards taking
a roundabout path of seldom used, wilderness
trails, carefully avoiding the larger
thoroughfares for my fear of being captured by
my fellow colonials and strung up at the
gallows terrified me far more than the prospect
of losing my scalp at the hands of the savages.
The overgrown and crooked trails through the
rocky, pine-forested Adirondack Mountains were
piled high with snow, a fact that contributed
to my mental as well as my physical anguish as
it was now impossible to move without leaving a
trail of solitary hoof marks in my wake, hoof
marks that bore the signature of Continental
Army horse shoes. It is only by the Grace of
God that I managed to evade—perhaps managed to
'luckily avoid' being the more appropriate
term—the roaming bands of Mohawks that polluted
the area as thickly as animal fodder piles on
the streets in Philadelphia. My stomach aching
with hunger, my body chilled to the core, I had
just unknowingly crossed the national border of
the State of Vermont[4] when I was suddenly jolted
out of my semi-conscious trance of bored misery
by a booming, "Halt, who goes there!"

A fur clad sentry, enormous in stature
with a height greater than six feet and
shoulders as broad as a bull's torso, appeared
before me brandishing an ancient musket.

"Two other muskets are trained on you from the
trees over there, hold still and state your
business in my country if you value your life!"
The sentry barked, splattering me with tobacco-
stained saliva as he spoke.

"I am Andrew Abbot, deserter from the colonial
war and a seeker of quarter." I replied

dishonestly, a moral failing that burned at my soul though my rational mind knew that I was in no position to afford the luxury of integrity.

"More and more of you every day, deserter. We got ourselves a damned army of deserters large enough to whoop on the New Yorkers if the politicians would let us. When was the last time you had something warm in your belly, Sir?" The sentry said with a smile as tobacco juice trickled down his prominently jutting chin. "By the way you talk you must be an officer, probably Virginian or a Carolina man, am I right?"

"Yes, a former officer." I replied as I made a mental note to stop slurring my speech in the Virginian fashion as it was better for strangers not to have such an obvious clue as to my history. "I've added two notches to my belt since leaving," I confessed to the sentry, "and I can't remember the last time I had a decent meal."

4. The State of Vermont was located between The Colony of New York and The Colony of New Hampshire on land that was claimed by both—claims that were stringently rejected by the militantly independent Vermonters. The Vermonters took advantage of the outbreak of the Revolution as an opportunity to formally declare their independence, a fact that nearly turned the colonial revolution into a civil war between the northern colonies. Though the Continental Congress refused to recognize their state, the Vermonters initially allied themselves with the Continentals. Vermonters Ethan Allen and his Green Mountain Boys led the early colonial victory at Fort Ticonderoga, a stunning triumph over the British that nearly led King George III into insanity. Yet the relationship between Vermont and its more powerful former master, New York, continued to sour with loud calls by the New York delegation to the Continental Congress for action by the Continental Army against the rogue republic. The Vermonters responded by hunkering down in their mountains, hostile to Patriot and British soldier alike, openly welcoming deserters from either army to join their ranks.

I dismounted my half-starved stallion and allowed the sentry to lead me to the Vermonter's camp, a small collection of tents centered about a large cave at the base of a pine-speckled, boulder-strewn, snow-covered mountain, a mount larger and more beautiful than any of the peaks I ever witnessed in the ranges that occupy Virginia's western frontiers. I followed the sentry into the cave where I found four towering, sinewy men dressed in frontier's garb, none of the men less than six foot in height, a fact that astounded me for at five-foot-ten I was considered a tall man in Virginia. A fifth man was standing in the cave a few feet back from the others, an Indian dressed in white man's clothing. With brown eyes and a mean scowl, the Indian looked to be a vicious warrior and I wondered what tribe, and of how many numbers, had allied with the Vermont Republic, praying silently that this Indian was not a Mohawk. The Vermonters were huddled around an aged and splintering table that was missing one of its legs, the leg having been replaced by an axe handle that had been crudely wedged into the plateau. Their table was covered in large military maps with pebbles and pieces of tree bark lying scattered on top to represent the current location of both Vermonter and enemy units. The Vermont sentry announced my presence and the men at the table looked up, uniformly appearing displeased at the interruption, the most senior man answering the sentry in a cantankerous voice, "why bring him here, you fool, take him to the Sergeant Major like all of the others!"

"But Major O'Dea, Sir, this one is an officer, Sir." The sentry replied nervously, an unnatural look of fear skirting across the bearish man's rugged face.

"Very well, have him wait outside." The Major ordered with a noncommittal wave of his hand

before returning his attention back to his
battle map.

The Vermont sentry and I exited the cave
and shivered in the snow for hours, waiting
impatiently and cursing the weather, our misery
compounded greatly by the ferocious winds that
swept down the mountain, winds channeled to our
location by the mountain's crooks into gusts of
tempestuous fury. As the sentry and I were
contemplating building a fire for warmth, I was
finally beckoned back inside the Vermonters'
headquarters by a young Lieutenant, who
dismissed my frostbitten guard back to his
outpost.

"Major O'Dea, Sir, I am Captain Andrew Abbot
and I am grateful for your quarter." I said,
bowing my head slightly in deference and
offering the Major my hand.

"Abbot hmmm, I imagine you were born as much an
Abbot as I was born an O'Dea…unfortunate how
war can turn honest men into liars. I joined
the Army of Vermont after the invasion of
Canada, that great epic failure of military
judgment. I was one of the few survivors of
that damned fool's crusade. Now I fight for
myself, independent of both Royal tyranny and
the colonial arrogance of the damned New
Yorkers, New Yorkers whose congressional
delegation continues to try to force General
Washington to invade Vermont to this very day.
We are a ragtag bunch: native Vermonters,
Continental and Royal Army deserters, and even
a tribe of natives who have grown as weary of
the Iroquois' civil war as I have of the
continental revolt. Our numbers are small but
we fight on the ground of our choosing, high in
the mountains, ambushing the enemy whenever he
is foolish enough to trespass along our
mountain trails. This strategy has allowed us
to defeat the much larger forces of our foes
time and again. Indeed, we have humbled the

bastards with such regularity that we have won
ourselves a de facto peace with both the Royal
and Continental Armies—for the time being
anyhow. At present our greatest threats are the
Mohawk and Seneca tribes, their naturally
aggressive tendencies stoked by the New Yorkers
who are actively inciting the Indians against
us in spite of General Washington's explicit
disapproval. That is our situation. Now, tell
me of yourself Captain Abbot, are you passing
through or are you looking to join our army?"

        I hesitated, unsure of how much
information I should divulge for I was well
aware that I had a large price on my head and
an executioner eagerly awaiting my return. Yet
I knew that it would be impossible to traverse
Vermont without trusting this man, at least
partly trusting him anyhow. I was a foreigner
in these rugged and dangerous lands that were
capable of killing a man in a thousand
different ways and I wouldn't make it without
assistance.

"I am passing through to Quebec City where I
hope to find passage to Europe." I replied with
frankly.

"Passage to Europe! You surprise me, Captain
Abbot, I would never have taken you for a
murderer!" The Major retorted. Yes, it must be
murder for a man to risk fleeing the continent
in this age of warfare, warfare that is even
more barbaric at sea than it is here in the
mountains. No matter, it's the promise of a
man's future that concerns me, not the history
of his rotting past." Major O'Dea said through
a bemused smile that now crossed his heavily
bearded face.

"I have no food and I would greatly appreciate
any quarter that you might be willing to offer.
I have some money, but it must last me all the
way to Canada. How long is the ride to Quebec

City, Sir, and what is the best route for a man who wishes to avoid official inquiry?" I asked, silently praying that the Vermonters would at least offer me a warm meal to fill my aching belly.

"This time of year, God only knows how long the ride will take you over these icy paths. The backwoods trails are prohibitively treacherous in the winter and the main roads are of no use to you as they are constantly traversed by trespassing British and Colonials invaders and frequently ambushed by the Indian hostiles." Replied the Major, his words less than encouraging. "Regardless, the St. Lawrence River is dangerously iced throughout the winter months, with strong and unpredictable currents lying just beneath. You won't be able to find passage on a sea-going vessel until April, perhaps late March if the weather is on your side. Let me speak bluntly, Captain Abbot. My regiment is painfully short on officers. I have plenty of eager musketmen but few men of quality to lead them. Why not join us until the spring and fatten your stomach and your wallet before leaving for Canada—perhaps kill a few Continentals or Indians for sport while you wait for the spring thaw?"

"Are you offering me a commission, Sir?" I inquired, somewhat incredulously.

"If you'll accept it, then I'm offering, Son. If the answer's 'no' then I'm not offering." Major O'Dea responded crisply, his hands on his hips and demanding an immediate answer.

"Then I will gladly accept your generous proposal, Sir, and pray that I do not disappoint you." I replied with a smile of happy surprise as we shook hands violently.

"Good, then go fetch yourself a hardy plate of rations, you look like a scarecrow." My generous new commander ordered. "I will have you introduced you to your men later this evening."

I followed the potent waft of smoking rations to the mess pit where I helped myself to a warm plate of highly piled dinner rations that consisted of heavily salted ham hocks, flame-charred potatoes, and overly-crisped turnips that would have caused my gut to protest under any other circumstance, but given my famished condition, tasted like a wedding feast to my wanting tongue. The next day, I was placed in charge of a company of Vermonters—twenty hardened fighting men, experts in mountain warfare. My company, which was barely the size of a Continental Army platoon, was divided into two small platoons of ten men apiece, each platoon led by a Sergeant in lieu of a Lieutenant due to the severe shortage of officers in the Vermont Militia. First platoon was led by Sergeant First Class Beaver Fox, a Mahican Indian who was in exile from his native New York due to unrelenting Mohawk aggression against his tribe, a tribe which had suffered the misfortune of fighting on the weaker of the warring sides in the brutal Iroquois civil war. A colorful Irish Canadian, Sergeant First Class Thomas McCloud, commanded second platoon, which being entirely composed of British Army deserters was a tightly knit fraternity of martial brethren who especially enjoyed a good fight with the Royal Army whenever the British commanders foolishly choose to cross into Vermont from British Canada during their frequent raids against New York Colonials. Overall, my first impression of my new command was pleasantly favorable and I settled into my role as company commander seamlessly, beginning an intensive training regimen the very next day to improve my unit's discipline and combat effectiveness. It wasn't long before I was leading the most respected, and the most deadly, company in the Vermont militia.

January 1779: My Vermonters and I were involved in constant irregular engagements, engagements undertaken partly to fulfill our duty to The State of Vermont, and partly because my soldiers, like myself, were filled with the boiling rage of the forsaken, an emotional burden that transformed us into an unstoppable fighting machine with an insatiable thirst for combat. As the winter weeks grew into months, and quite to my surprise, I found myself developing an especially strong friendship with Sergeant First Class Beaver Fox, a man who spoke the English language fluently and without trace of an Indian accent. Beaver Fox's command of English was equally matched by his skill with the musket and the tomahawk; both weapons were perpetually at his side and ready to be used at a moment's notice. I shall never forget the conversation he and I shared whilst cooking our rations over the campfire as we relaxed after a minor engagement with a Mohawk war party the evening of January 28th, 1779.

"You're men fight bravely, very bravely, Sergeant." I complemented with utmost sincerity for Beaver Fox's Mahican's were warriors of the highest quality.

"That is because we fight with hatred in our hearts, Sir. We try to squelch the burden of the war by avenging the deaths of our people with Mohawk blood, but I fear that the emptiness we all feel inside will never leave us and that it will continue to haunt the pathetic remnants of the once proud Mahican Tribe until The Great Spirit mercifully grants us the ultimate peace, the silence of death."

"I feel like a fool, no, like a coldhearted scoundrel for not having asked you before, but why did the Mahicans flee to Vermont and why do you fight so willingly side-by-side with white men?" I queried with the greatest of interest.

"When the Iroquois Civil War erupted my people declared neutrality. My father, the eldest chief of the Mahicans, feared that war with the white men would destroy our profitable trading alliances so he refused to fight for either the revolutionaries or the British. My people had grown wealthy in commerce trading with the Colonials in Albany, Boston, and even Philadelphia and we became so enriched that many of the Mahican chiefs' sons were able to obtain university educations. I learned to speak English while in England, something I think no other Iroquois can claim. But my tribes' prosperity came at the expense of our warrior ethos, my people setting aside their tomahawks and their muskets for farm tools and trading wagons. The Mohawk attacked us without warning—scalping, pillaging, raping…not even sparing the children. My people, once plentiful, are now dying…so few of us are left and all of the chiefs are dead. But Mahican pride runs thick in our blood so we choose to fight on. Though our body is decapitated our heart still beats and our arms still swing the tomahawk for Mohawk scalps!" The stone-faced, stoic Sergeant First Class declared loudly, his eyes uncharacteristically animated and beaming with Mahican pride as he spoke. "I organized my people, those few who were left, and then fled to these mountains where I found the people of Vermont as wanting for musketmen as my people were for refuge from the Mohawk. My people now fight for the love of our new home, yes, but we also fight for the sweet taste of revenge!" My Platoon Sergeant forcefully gestured with his tomahawk as he spoke, swinging it and hacking into a thick tree branch, sending splinters flying through the air. "In my heart I realize that it is a fool's errand, this revenge, for our women and children are dead or are slaves of the Mohawk. The Mahican Tribe is dead and those of us who survive kill Mohawk only to lighten what little is left of our heavy hearts."

The Indian went silent, the emotion fading from his face, ashamed that he had shared so many of his most intimate thoughts with an outsider. We shared a long moment of silence, the stately Indian and I, as we slowly sipped our stout black Vermont ale.

"I have killed many Mohawk and I have never regretted it." I said frankly, shrugging my shoulders with indifference as I spoke.

"I hate the Mohawk in my heart, but in my soul I know that it is not the Mohawk who are evil; it is man's wars, man's greed..." A broad, toothy grin crept across Beaver Fox's stoic face, his solemn look of tortured wisdom disappearing for the briefest of moments "…but it still feels good to kill Mohawk!"

We burst into a fit of laughter, ale spewing from my lips onto my uniform, the sight of which compelled us to laugh even harder. Perhaps it was the strong ale, or perhaps the emotion of the moment, but I was overcome by a wave of complete fidelity in my valiant Platoon Sergeant and a simultaneously overwhelming urge to speak of the events that had haunted my dreams these past months, the terrible events that had brought me to Vermont. I trusted Beaver Fox with something I have never since confided to another human being, I trusted him with the story of my past—my crimes included—as the stoic Indian watched me sob, an emotional catharsis more healing than any cure prescribed by a physician, shaman, or saint. As I spoke and poured my dark emotions out as quickly as they would flow off of my trembling tongue, I felt as if a great boulder—a filthy, shameful boulder—had been lifted from my sagging, bruised shoulders and willfully held in the

Mahican Warrior's calloused hands, even if just for a moment. When I was done, unable to speak any further, Beaver Fox and I sipped mug after mug of ale in silence until we were as drunk as British seamen during a port call. Just before I passed out, overcome by the effects of the powerful Vermont brew, Beaver Fox put his hand on my shoulder and quietly said "you are my brother, Jonathan, and a member of the dying Mahican Nation."

30 January 1779: Eleven recruits arrived at our militia's camp, deserters from the Continental Army seeking quarter. Seven of the recruits were assigned to my company, a fact that I accepted with the greatest of reluctance given my present distain for all men who had ever believed in the Patriot mantra. My reservations aside, I could not deny the fact that my company was in dire need of reinforcement for we had suffered a disproportionately large number of casualties compared to the rest of the regiment, largely due to my soldier's, and my own, lust for combat. As I led the seven former Continentals from the regimental headquarters and back to my company's base camp, I made eye contact with one of the recruits and I thought, for the briefest of moments, that I recognized the man. If my new soldier recognized me his face betrayed nothing and I convinced myself to force this dark thought out of my mind, downplaying it as nothing more than another of my disturbingly frequent intrusions of paranoia. I introduced the recruits to their assigned platoons then gave a short, but heartfelt, motivational speech and then retired to my sleeping tent to plan tomorrow's ambushes. Weary from the previous night's gluttony of ale and fresh rations, I dozed off atop my favorite strategizing map, my face resting on my small maple wood desk as I slept hunched over, seated on my roughly nailed, pine wood stool.

Jarred from my slumber by a cold tickle against my face, I opened my eyes to find myself staring down the barrel of a French-made Continental Army musket. It took me a moment to register that I was indeed awake and confronted by reality, not dreaming away in one of the now habitual nightmares that had parasitized my sleep since my betrayal in the New York forests. Rubbing the sleep from my eyes, I found one of my new recruits standing at the end of the cocked musket and surrounded by his fellow conspirators. They forcefully accosted me while shouting, "this is a citizen's arrest and you is under arrest fer murder." I let loose a howl of desperation that echoed through the camp as my tormentors manhandled me from my tent towards a waiting horse-drawn wagon, my escort to the executioner's noose.

"CRACK, CRACK, CRACK!"

Three musket shots rang out, the muzzle blasts piercing the pitch black of the night and temporarily blinding me as I felt the shockwaves from the lead balls whizzing past my body. My night vision recovering and I saw three of my captors pummeling like pinecones from a tree onto the frosty ground, the life exiting their bodies as their trembling comrades panicked and fled into the woods like a family of wild hares being chased by a pack of famished hounds. My rescuers emerged from behind the curtain of gun smoke, a squad of Mahicans, their tomahawks drawn as they surrounded me in a defensive circle, Sergeant First Class Beaver Fox at their lead. Beaver Fox waved his tomahawk towards the woods and the Mahicans sprinted off to chase after my fleeing captors. The Mahican's tomahawks thirsted for blood as they pursued the treacherous Colonials out of sight and into the depths of the forest blacks. Beaver Fox patted me on my shoulder, a welcome gesture of reassurance to a man who was utterly shaken to his core, my body shivering with fear.

"Lucky that we were so close by, Jonathan…I have been watching those men all day and I knew that something was wrong about them. Your identity is revealed, my friend, it will not be long before other soldiers in the regiment attempt to ransom you for the bounty that you bear on your scalp. You must flee for Canada tonight, there is no time for delay." The great Indian said, his voice calm but assertive.

"You are the truest friend I have ever known and I am ashamed that I have spent so much of my life hating your people." I looked down as I spoke, sincerely remorseful for the prejudices of my past, prejudices that had blinded me to my Platoon Sergeant's inestimable valor for so long.

"All men fear that which is foreign to them, all men despise that which is different. My people and I are no exception to this unfortunate rule—it is the way of man. Look over there, my braves return with many scalps."

Beaver Fox called to his kinsmen in their harsh native tongue and demanded an immediate report, a report which he received with a look of displeasure etched into his face as he turned to me to translate.

"Two of the traitors escaped." Beaver Fox informed me regretfully. "You must leave now—the roads will be swarming with bounty hunters by daybreak as surely as the sun will rise. My braves and I will travel with you to the border, from there on I cannot help you."

I quickly stuffed my meager possessions into my trouser pockets, including the past two months pay, pay that had been thoughtfully paid in British gold by Major O'Dea who was fully

aware that Continental currency would be of no
use to me in Canada. Minutes later Beaver Fox,
two of his Mahican braves, and I mounted our
steeds and we sped off along the icy mountain
paths at such great speed that it bordered on
suicidal. Riding twenty hours a day, my Mahican
protectors were tireless as they drove me
forward, mercilessly shouting at me to stay
alert, our survival depending on every man's
wits as we traveled up-and-down the wind
chilled, snow covered, treacherously slippery
mountain passes. My moisture-impregnated
clothing provided hardly any protection against
the bite of the northern winds, winds which
seemed to blow straight through my body,
entering on one side and exiting the other,
leaching my precious body heat and pummeling me
with an unrelenting desire to fall asleep in my
saddle. In spite of these challenges, our
ragtag group succeeded in reaching the Canadian
border, a most welcome yet bittersweet
accomplishment. My Indian protectors and I
camped beside a warm fire that they kindled in
a secluded narrows that was walled by steep
cliffs, a shelter from the winds that allowed
us a blessed respite as we rested our exhausted
minds and bodies. After two days of lazy
rejuvenation, Beaver Fox presented me with his
tomahawk as a parting gift, a look of sadness
pasted over his rigid face. I bade my friend an
emotional farewell, knowing that I could never
repay his kindness and cognizant that I would
never again meet a man of his quality. As I
crossed into British Canada alone I paused for
a brief moment to glance back at my former
homeland, wondering if I would ever return. I
forced this troubling thought from my mind as I
spurred my horse onwards towards my
destination, the fortress-port of Quebec City.

CHAPTER 8
Crossing the Pond

Traveling northwards through the Canadian plains was uneventful thanks in large part to my Vermont mountain man's attire which blended perfectly with the style of clothing favored by the local French-Canadians. The few British patrols that I encountered ignored me, none of them even bothering to second a glance as I rode past them in silence. My boyhood French lessons, lessons which I had vocally protested against as a schoolboy in Virginia, proved invaluable as I was able to conjure up enough French to barter for room-and-board at the local inns, inns which were plentiful—a source of scarce income for French-Canadian farmers during the long northern winters. I was a bit hesitant at first to risk exposing myself so openly but after risking a few quick meals at passing bed-and-breakfasts I grew so confident in the French-Canadian's disdain for the British Crown that my fears of innkeeper's possibly turning me over to the King's authorities soon became a distant afterthought. The snow-covered Canadian roadways were lined by row-after-row of deeply frosted farm fields, an occasional patch of evergreens disrupting the monotony, though interrupting it far too seldom as I rode through the snowy nothingness in absolute solitude, desperate for any distraction from the memories of my past that mercilessly rampaged through my unoccupied mind.

As the days turned into weeks, I had begun to think that the frozen tundra would never end when I suddenly spotted the great fortress city, the capital of French Canada, against the pale horizon. Quebec City sat preening upon steep bluffs that overlooked the mighty St. Lawrence River, the river that served as the French-Canadian colony's lifeline to the mighty Atlantic Ocean, that great highway of trade and travel upon which the globe-spanning power of the British Empire rested. Atop the bluffs stood the city's mighty inner walls, ornate walls of French design that had been substantially augmented by a lacing of modern outer ramparts of British construct that were erected after the French and Indian War by Quebec City's new Anglican masters. It was against these very same city walls that Benedict Arnold's Colonial Army had been butchered like a herd of cattle in a slaughter house by blazing British musket and cannon fire during the disastrous winter invasion of in 1775. General Arnold's failure had been a great setback for the Continental Army for it was through Canada that Britain supplied its Northern Army, an army that presented an ever looming threat to the New England Colonies' western flanks, a threat which prevented General Washington from concentrating the entirety of his forces against the Crown's great stronghold in New York City.

March 1779: I entered Quebec City and found lodging at a cheap Inn that was located above a raucous French brothel, the smell of fornication wafting through the establishment so putridly that I had difficulty sleeping my first night. Though I had a purse full of gold, I knew that any captain audacious enough to sell passage to Europe to a strange foreigner during this age of warfare would demand a hefty price, so I guarded my coins as jealously as a bulldogge bitch hovers over her newborn pups. It proved to be an early thawing and the might St. Lawrence's ice melted weeks ahead of local expectations, a fact that was celebrated loudly by Quebec's deep sea fishermen who were already bustling about preparing their vessels for the sea, the harbor ringing with the harsh staccato of hammer-against-nail and the dull grating of saw-against-plank. I surveyed the city's harbor for several weeks, carefully observing the regulars as they came and went about their business, making a mental list of those persons whose behavior suggested that their professional interests might lie in something other than fishing, namely contraband smuggling. Surprisingly, these clandestine smugglers were quite easy to identify for they operated in the open with no evident fear of the law. The explanation for the smugglers' seeming immunity from British authority, though elusive to me at first, became stunningly apparent during a daytrip to the shopping district. While browsing for a new pair of clothes, an outfit more befitting of a city dweller than my current frontiersman's garb, I found the streets overflowing with British officers escorting local ladies, ladies that were dressed in the latest and finest Parisian fashions, clothing that had surely been purchased illegally for a full embargo of French goods had been instituted by the Royal Navy at the outbreak of official hostilities between the two mighty nations. I strolled past the lavishly dressed pairs of lovers and purchased a set of urban wear. I then set off for the dock with a smile upon my face, knowing that it was time for a conversation with the French-Canadian smugglers.

Captain Georges Rafael was a tough-as-nails, middle-aged seaman with a sun hardened face and a Frenchman's pointy chin that proudly sported a neatly kept goatee beard in accordance with the latest French fashion. The Captain's heavily muscled and crudely tattooed arms were bulging from his sleeves, sleeves that he wore exceedingly short, indeed so short that they barely covered his shoulders in blunt defiance of the chill air that continued to cloak Quebec City even under the rays of the apical sun. Sitting in a salty tavern across from the docks, I watched Captain Rafael bark profanity-woven orders to his crew, a rugged looking bunch of seamen, even by smuggler's standards. The crew swarmed about the Captain's smallish, yet solidly constructed swoop, *Le Bourbon*, with half of the men removing the ship's wintering while the other half rhythmically loaded prodigious quantities of provisions—these men were clearly preparing for a lengthy voyage—whilst loudly singing vulgar seaman's songs. The sun began its terminal descent at three-thirty in the afternoon and the sailors set aside their tools and followed their captain into the tavern where I sat. They barreled past my booth as they entered from the cold, the potent smell of the kegs of salted ham and smoked fish rations that they had been loading filling the air. I nervously sipped my fifth cup of coffee and nibbled at my meal—my third since entering the tavern, much to the barkeeper's delight—while staring intently at the same crumpled news pamphlet that I had been pretending to read all day, biding my time and hoping to catch the captain alone for a private conversation.

The crew of *Le Bourbon* shattered the tavern's silence with loud demands for beer and brandy, drinks which the barkeeper hurriedly provided in generous quantities, sliding mugs of thick Canadian ale down the counter, vessels which were drained by the eager sailors before the heads of their brews had had time to settle. As his crewmen drank themselves warm and merry with alcohol, Captain Rafael sat in solitude, slowly savoring his meal of grilled arctic salmon, French bread, and tomato stew with a glass of dark red wine, his untrusting eyes darting from side-to-side as he kept close watch on every soul in his proximity.

With no further reason for delay, out of excuses for further procrastination, I forced myself to swallow my anxiety and to summon the courage to rise from my seat and approach the fearsome smuggler. Captain Rafael raised his head cautiously as I neared, his expression darkening, his thick brow creasing into great furrows, the jagged purple scar on his cheek blanching as his right hand slipped beneath the table into his waistband where a pistol was concealed, poorly concealed, its brass and polished wood handle visible from clear across the tavern.

"Bon Jour, Capitan." I greeted the captain, my voice light and spoken through a cautious smile.

"Bon Jour." Captain Rafael replied flatly, his hand wrapped tightly around his pistol, his eyes communicating a willingness to use the weapon should he become so inclined.

As I began to bumble about in my broken French the captain tersely interjected, "I speak English! Spent me childhood runnin' rum in the Caribbean, now what the hell do you want?"

"May I have a seat, please?" I asked politely, my hands shaking, unnerved by the man's uncouth demeanor but in no position to be offended by it.

"Tell me what the bloody hell you want before I sit you down on the floor with lead in your chest!" Captain Rafael scowled menacingly.

"I was hoping to buy safe passage to Europe, France if possible." I replied, my voice sturdy, determined not to reveal the fear that was jolting down my spine.

"There is no safe passage across the sea these days, boy." The captain responded as he sat back in his chair and slightly relaxed the grip on his pistol.

"Passage then," I suggested as I sat myself in the chair across from him without invitation, praying that this would not prove to be a fatal miscalculation.

The captain returned to his meal, chewing several sloppy bites, ignoring me as he pondered my proposition. His mouth full of salmon, the captain finally replied with a spit laden, "It'll cost you thirty guineas an' not a farthing less."

The price was highway robbery. I full well knew that passage across the Atlantic before the war cost no more than ten guineas, less for a man of character who commanded the proper connections. Yet I also knew that I had no other options and that, thanks to the generosity of the State of Vermont, this outrageous sum was nonetheless within my financial means.

"I'm good for the sterling, Captain." I responded slowly and after a good while of pretending to weigh his offer, though in reality I was so desperate for passage that I would have accepted an extortion even more brazen than the one that the was being demanding.

"Then show me your coins or make yourself rare with a light step. I'm in an ill-temper, ya see." The captain drawled, talking downward towards his food with his mouth full, not bothering to shift his gaze up in my direction.

Insulted, I swallowed the pride that ran thick in my Virginian blood and I opened my purse before the captain. He grunted in approval at the sight of my guineas as he continued to devour his meat.

"We leave in two days, departin' at dawn n' not a tick o' the clock later, you on board er' otherwise. Give me half'er the gold now, the other half'er be due when we's gets ta France."

"I'll provide the first installment of the agreed price the morning of our departure, no sooner." I replied forcefully, praying that the captain wouldn't call my bluff.

The captain responded with a noncommittal grunt as he waved me away with his large battle-calloused hand, once again returning to his meal and taking a large bite of the scaly salmon that pummeled with his golden teeth, his mouth wide open. I turned to leave the tavern, now full of pessimism and thinking that I had failed when the captain loudly barked after me, spraying a foul mixture of food and wine as he yelled.

"Remember boy, don't be late 'cause I ain't waitin' for ya none, hear me now!"

My spirits lifted like a saint's soul during the rapture and I set off for the shopping district where I sold my stallion to a horse trader for a fair price, hoping that the honest stallion wouldn't find his next employment behind a field plough or underneath the grinding stone at the local glue factory. I strolled through the frost-chilled night back to my inn and then set about writing to my poor family, writing a letter of farewell.

Dear Beloved Family,

I am well and missing you dearly. Please forgive me for the shame that I have cast upon our sacred family name and upon the honor of the Great State of Virginia. I will not beg you to excuse my abhorrent behavior, but I do heartfully request that you bear in mind that there are two sides to every story, including mine, and that I am not the monster that the

news pamphlets would make me out to be. I am
resigned to the fact that I must leave the
colonies, likely never to return, to protect
what little of our reputation I have not
already managed to desecrate. I miss you all so
very much.

Your Prodigal Son,
Jonathan

April 1779: The morning the second of April was
bitter cold and thickly overcast. The sticky,
low hanging blanket of sea fog encapsulated the
harbor so entirely that it was only by light of
the deck torches that I was able to find my way
to *Le Bourbon* as I wandered aimlessly down the
narrow, unlit streets that led to the misty
wharfs. As I neared the smugglers' moored
vessel, I called out for the captain who
answered through the fog with a sharp command
to board immediately. On *Le Bourbon's* creaky
deck I found the captain standing with his
brawny skull-and-dagger tattooed arms crossed
in front of his barrel chest, the frightening
man now in even a fouler mood than he had been
in yesterday.

"Lucky ya' arrived so early. Ya' almost missed
yer transpert' and it's a long swim 'cross the
Atlantic fer a man without fins." Captain
Rafael slurred his speech, a half-cocked smile
wrinkling his crusty face, the smell of last
night's drink still thick on his breath.

"But sunrise isn't for three more hours." I
retorted defensively.

"Some damned ambitious fool has gone an' taken
himself command a' the Brit fleet while the
admiral's gone away supportin' the army down
south. This young bastard commander, he's
decided ta' harass us seamen, tryin' real hard
to make a name fer himself, ya see." The

captain said with a dark laugh that was quickly
followed by a condescending grunt of defiance.
"This new big man, he just set fire ta' the
ship o' a friend a' me yesterdays, no more n'
twenty minutes after da' poor dead bastard
dropped his moorin'; may he reach the Gates o'
St. Peter 'fore the Devil knows his corpse is
rotted!"

"And what of his crew?" I inquired with real
concern for I was well aware that any more than
a few moments in the frigid Canadian waters
would freeze a man's blood thick and suck the
life from his body.

"They's all's dead, every single one of um';
froze in the waters where the British left um'.
The British watched um' slip under slow into
the deep. They shot a few I hears, like geeses
on a pond they did. The fancy English sailors
was all braggin' bout' it at the tavern after
ya' departed." The captain grunted with a dark
grin. "One's who was shot, them was the lucky
ones 'cause they died quick and painless."

"Are we still sailing then?" I demanded, my
heart filling with the fear that my escape
attempt was coming to naught with freedom so
nearly within my grasp.

"Aye, we cast off momentarily. God willin' the
darkness will protect us, the darkness an' the
speed of this fine ship o' me. This good ship
have saved me sorry old ass more'n once er'
twice before nows." Captain Rafael quipped, his
mood improving.

     The Captain barked orders like a rabid
dog, moving his crewmen about the ship like a
chess master pushing his pawns across the
board, ordering them to throw off the bowline
and to unfurl *Le Bourbon's* three great masts.
With the sails now flapping in the strong winds
overhead, the captain ordered that all of his

ship's cannon be loaded and prepared for action. Captain Rafael made a final survey of the decks, and finding the ship to be in good order, barked a command to "commence rowin'" to the dozen crewmen that sat in the twin long boats that were to drag *Le Bourbon* off of the wharf and into the river. The men began rowing and the thick lines that attached their longboats to the bow creaked as they were pulled taut. *Le Bourbon* hesitated for a moment, as stubborn a ship as the man who commanded her, then slowly began edging her way in into the St. Lawrence River.

Le Bourbon was an elegantly crafted sloop with a low profile to the sea that made her difficult to spot on the open ocean and that also contributed greatly to her speed, which was nearly on par with the fastest British Man O' War in ideal seas. She bore nine cannon on both her port and starboard in addition to a pair of smaller, swiveling deck cannon that stood perched atop the bow and the stern for a total of twenty cannon in the ship's entire complement. Adding to this formidable artillery array was a plethora of muskets, pistols, and sabers that the crew wore tucked haphazardly in their belts as casually as townsmen wear their hats and wigs. The waters of the St. Lawrence, narrow and turbulent at the Port of Quebec, rapidly widened into a broad, white-capped bay that then transitioned into the expanses of the mighty Atlantic. *Le Bourbon* sailed towards the open sea at a frightful pace, powered by a powerful northern wind propelling her from the aft. As the last vestiges of land vanished out of sight, I turned to Captain Rafael to congratulate him over his ship's fine performance when suddenly a frigate's mainmast peaked over the horizon.

"Damn this Devil's gale, we can out run them in any other wind but not if the sea keeps tossing me little ship about like a babe's toy in the washtub. The bigger the ship, the better she handles in the high wind, ya see. Hard fer a little fellar like us ta' keep a steady course but that Man O' War won't have her no trouble, she won't!" The captain cursed our luck, muttering profanities that were lost into the vicious tempest.

"We have a sizable lead; they'll have to work hard to overtake us." I suggested with cautious optimism.

"A lead we has indeed, thanks ter me. I had some a' me fishin' mates put ta' sea just 'fore we sailed as a diversion. That's why we wasn't stopped leavin' the port." Captain Rafael lectured professorially with the eerie calm of a man who was no stranger to maritime peril.

"If they catch us, will there be a fight?" I begged with my gaze fixated downwards onto the ferociously whipped sea that sprayed over "Le Bourbon's" bow as we descended into a wave's cavernous trough. The frigid ocean spray drenched my clothing straight through in the icy sea water, a potent reminder of my imminent fate if *Le Bourbon* were to go down in the Atlantic.

"Aye, there will be." The captain replied with the aggressive determination of a boxer preparing for a title match, his knuckles gripped white around his ornate, gold-décor, ruby-studded looking glass.

"Then I'll be requiring a weapon, Sir!" I said loudly, determined that if fate would have me die this bitter day I would die fighting, falling from pistol shot or saber slash rather than swinging from the gallows.

Captain Raphael sent me below to his private quarters, trusting me with the key to his battered sea chest, a chest which I found to be full of sabers, pistols, powder, and shot. I loaded four pistols and tucked them beneath my belt, two pistols on my front and another two in the rear against the small of my back. I selected a long, curved Arabian scythe from the captain's bladed collection and then I slammed the trunk shut, its shiny lock clanking loudly, the ring echoing through the hull. I returned to the deck to await my destiny as a man of honor, determined not to be taken alive like a cowardly peasant, even if it meant dying fighting side-by-side with buccaneer scoundrels. The enemy frigate, now within range of cannon shot, unfurled a great banner and I was shocked to behold the red, white, and blue flag of the Continental Congress.

"It be a Yankee frigate!" Captain Rafael shouted to his crew, his intonation betraying the fact that the captain was just as surprised as I.

"This far north?" I exclaimed in disbelief.

"Aye, huntin' fer royal shippin' and gainin' fast ta' our stern." The captain growled as he folded his looking glass shut and unsheathed his saber.

Captain Rafael barked to the crew to aim their cannon as the *Le Bourbon's* sharpshooters scurried to man the sniper perches atop the violently swaying masts. The colonial frigate neared, the enemy captain holding his fire in anticipation of delivering a devastating initial barrage, its massive silhouette looming down upon *Le Bourbon* like the shadow of the Angel of Death. The Yankee frigate, hardly two ship lengths away, maneuvered to deliver a fatal broadside but Captain Rafael deftly weaved *Le Bourbon* back-and-forth on the sea, frustrating the frigate's best efforts to align herself in parallel with our ship, keeping *Le Bourbon's* stern directly in line with the Yankee interceptor's bow and thus preventing the enemy frigate from letting loose a definitive volley from its iron rows of port and starboard cannon. The colonial frigate closed to pistol range, the faces of its eager crew visible across the decks. With the speed and precision of a surgeon amputating a rotten limb, Captain Rafael swung *Le Bourbon* to the portside while his cannon simultaneously unleashed a thunderous volley that tore through the starboard wall of the Yankee frigate, sending great chunks of the enemy vessel's planking flying through the air. Then the frigate's powder stores burst into a great wall of fire that erupted through her deck, showering me in splinters as I fell to *Le Bourbon's* deck in panic, covering my head and neck with my arms, a large ballistic fragment of the colonial frigate's deck piercing my shoulder as I descended.

I scrambled to my feet, ignoring the warm blood that was trickling down my sleeve, following Captain Raphael and his buccaneers as they stormed across an unstable boarding plank onto the deck of the Yankee ship. Captain Rafael's crew mercilessly slaughtered every colonial in sight, the frigate's crewmen were too shocked from the explosion of their powder stores to offer any resistance as they were slain, the buccaneer's sabers dripping wet with the blood of dozens of enemy sailors before the smoke had begun to clear. I personally felled three colonials with my pistols and then I ran an unfortunate soul through his back with my scythe—a baby faced Lieutenant who had been attempting to make his way to one of the frigate's deck cannon. The crew of the enemy frigate retreated down their hatches but they would find no mercy in the bowels of their doomed ship. The outlaw sailors of the *Le Bourbon* held the frigate's crew at bay with musket fire, forcing the colonials, who had now realized the error of their judgment, back from the hatch doors and trapping them in the hull below. Captain Rafael directed his men to pour the enemy's powder kegs over their deck, a sadistic grin plastered on his face as his men laced the Yankee ship from bow-to-stern with black powder trails of death. Satisfied that their work was completed, Captain Rafael shouted a booming order to retreat and we sprinted back to the *Le Bourbon*, leaping the four foot gap between the two ships with the greatest of enthusiasms as the captain dropped a torch onto our foe's powder strewn deck. Safely back aboard his sloop, Captain Rafael ordered the sails unfurled with all possible speed and the *Le Bourbon* bobbed away over the choppy seas, a great inferno erupting on the Yankee frigate in the near distance, the screams of her crew echoing across the pitiless sea.

CHAPTER 9
Drunken Enlistment

September 1779: Marseilles, France. The French
hostel was small, dirty, and crowded; the
floors strewn with empty bottles of cheap
brandy and the stench of alcohol misting the
air, intertwining with the thick smoke of
second-rate cigars and the putrid wisp of
fermenting urine. I lay on my lice-infested
bunk staring at the news pamphlet that I had
nailed into the ceiling above my bunk, reading
of the exploits of my brother Henry for what
must have been the hundredth time, my heart
burning with jealousy. I gritted my teeth as I
read that they now called him, 'Light Horse
Harry', a moniker given by his troop of
dragoons[5] after he had led a valiant bayonet
charge at the Battle of Paulus Hook, killing
fifty British infantry and capturing one
hundred and fifty more whilst losing only half
a dozen of his own men. Yes, I thought, Light
Horse Harry was a revolutionary hero while his
brother was a pathetic drunkard rotting away in
an infested rat hole, a rat hole in the
underbelly of a the godforsaken, gluttonous,
popish Kingdom of France. Hating myself, I
contemplated suicide yet again, an ever present
thought that plagued my mind like a parasitic
mushroom feeding off of a sickly tree. I cursed
myself aloud, my bunkmates too drunk to pay me
any notice as I loudly rummaged through my
blankets for another bottle of brandy, the
second of the day, which I finished in one deep
burning swig, the caustic liquid searing my
throat as it trickled its way down to my rotted

5. Dragoons: Soldiers who rode into battler on
    horseback but who primarily fought dismounted. Used
    extensively in the American War of Independence by
    both of the warring sides for their superior
    mobility on the battlefield.

gut. I leapt off my bunk onto the hard, cold floor and dressed myself for the first time in a week, my clothes unwashed and stiffened with grim, grim that had been transformed into a stiff cement by my incessant drunkard's sweat. Fully clothed, it was now time to replenish my stock of liquor, the only reason I ever found now to leave my self-imposed prison. I swayed down the refuse strewn, sunbaked boulevards towards the local market where I barged through the door of the nearest pharmacy and fumbled about in my pocketbook for one of my few remaining gold coins. I purchased five bottles of the cheapest of the store's discounted brandies and a copy of the local news pamphlet, the clerk nodding to me with a sarcastically knowing smile as I handed him my payment.

Sipping the foul brandy, my sole source of nourishment for the past two months, I strained to decipher the news pamphlet, giving up on most stories before I could decipher them, my French as poor now as it had been on the day that I arrived. I had just reached the last page, the words beginning to jumble as my eyes blurred with intoxication, when my attention was suddenly caught by an advertisement placed by a Portuguese mercenary troop seeking to hire men with combat experience for an expedition to the distant land of Ling Chao. I hadn't the vaguest idea of where Ling Chao might lie on the map, save for that it was likely somewhere in the Orient, a region of the world notorious for killing men foolish enough to venture there, knocking them dead either by the hot fevers of tropical malady or the cold iron of the sword. I mumbled to myself drunkenly, "damn it all to hell, better to die as a fighting soldier than as a forgotten beggar," then I fell into unconsciousness onto my filthy linens. The next morning I packed my ever so meager belongings into my knapsack and then set off on the long hike to Lisbon, hitching rides by horseback or

buggy when I could, but pounding the
cobblestone and gravel with my blistered feet
more often than not, tracking over the snow-
covered Pyrenees Mountains from France into the
Iberian Peninsula then down the well-kept roads
of the Kingdoms of Spain and Portugal.

November 1779: Lisbon, Portugal. The crown
jewel of the globe-spanning Portuguese
commercial empire sat atop steep hills that
rapidly transitioned into pristine white sand
beaches that terminated into the deep turquoise
sea. The Bay of Lisbon sparkled in the sunlight
which bathed the sun-soaked city's
Mediterranean architecture and brilliantly
accentuated the bold red-pinks and aqua-blues
of the commercial edifices and the residential
dwellings. I strolled through the narrow,
winding streets and alleyways, streets where
there seemed to be as many merchants as there
were customers clogging the sides. The
merchantmen loudly hawked their exotic fares,
shouting to potential customers in the musical
Portuguese tongue, hawking fares that hailed
from darkest corners of the globe. I made my
way towards the northern wharfs as specified in
the advertisement that I had carried with me in
my breast pocket all of the way from France.

        The northern docks were located in a
downtrodden sector of Lisbon, the streets of
which were lined with dilapidated buildings,
the street corners crowded with rowdy pubs and
filthy brothels. Seductively dressed
prostitutes advertised their trade openly on
the dangerous streets and the stench of urine
hung in the air, courtesy of drunken sailors
who were to be found haphazardly slumped-over
in stupors of intoxication against every
building and lamppost in sight. Frigate-after-
frigate bearing the flags of every conceivable
nationality lined the harbor with their
national banners proudly flailing from their
mainmasts, each ship guarded by stone-faced

marines who were armed with musketoons that
were loaded with nails and buckshot, brightly
shining sabers sheathed smartly at their sides.
After a good bit of wandering, I found the ship
that I was searching for tied to an aging pier,
the Portuguese frigate *Sao Rafael*. I beckoned
to the *Sao Rafael's* deck guard and begged
permission to board in both French and English,
neither of which registered with the olive-
skinned Portuguese marine. Exasperated, I
resorted to hand signals and, with some
hesitation, the marine waved me aboard. I
crossed the creaking boarding plank, careful
not to fall into the shallow, refuse polluted,
rocky depths below. I stepped onto the
frigate's spit-shined deck which was crowded
with crates full of fresh produce, the hallmark
of a ship that was imminently preparing to
sail. The Portuguese marine led me into the
frigate's master chambers where I found the
captain of the *Sao Rafael* hard at work
sharpening an emerald-studded dirk against a
small grinding stone, a chalice of dark red
wine by his side. The captain looked up and
addressed me in broken and heavily accented
English as he continued to sharpen his blade,
the captain likely assuming my ethnicity and
native tongue based on the fairness of my skin,
hair, and eyes.

"Boss of company…Mr. Jacobs…he no here…return
soon." The captain informed me in a barely
intelligible slur.

The captain offered me a glass of port
wine[6], a fortified alcohol long popular with
sailors and made famous worldwide as the drink
of the freely-imbibing seamen of the British
Royal Navy. I eagerly accepted the port, having
run out of money a week prior, a period of
unintentional sobriety that my jittery nerves
were loudly protesting, drenching my palms in
sweat and afflicting me with a fine tremor. The
wine had barely touched my eager palate when

Mr. Jacobs waltzed into the room, filling the air with the calmly assertive demeanor of a man who was accustomed to getting his way. Mr. Jacob's was an Englishmen of hardy stock who towered overhead at six feet and three inches in height. He had long steely arms that were the size of municipal water pipes and his legs were akin to small tree trunks, legs that supported a barrel torso and a portly belly that betrayed Mr. Jacobs' great love affair with meat pie. He wore a finely crafted suit constructed of Italian silk that, in spite of the obviously high quality of its fabric, nevertheless managed to appear comical hanging over Mr. Jacobs' gorilla-sized frame.

"Voce tem um convidado, Excelentissimo Senhor." The Portuguese captain reported to his employer as he stood and rendered Mr. Jacobs an elegant bow.

"Obrigado, Ramon." Mr. Jacobs replied in turn as he spun about to face me, offering me his

6. Port Wine: A red wine made from grapes grown in the Douro Valley of northern Portugal and named after the city of Oporto, the region's major sea port. Port wine is fortified with twenty percent brandy, a fact that allows it to survive long sea voyages without spoiling whilst simultaneously increasing its alcohol content, two reasons for port wine's popularity on sailing ships. Port wine is found ubiquitously on the world-traveling ships of the British Royal Navy due to its relative cheapness in Britain compared to the wines of other countries, largely owing to a highly favorable trade agreement, the Methuen Treaty, signed between Britain and Portugal in 1703. The Methuen Treaty allows Britain access to cheap wine, wine which during the latter half of the 18th Century was in short supply due to the war with France, whilst guaranteeing British merchants favorable trading status in Lisbon. The treaty is an extension of a close alliance between Britain and Portugal that dates to 1373, when the two nations signed a treaty of 'perpetual friendship.

right hand while saying, "state your name and business, Son."

"I am Jonathan E. Lee, former captain of the Continental Army, and I am here to request your consideration for employment in the militia that you are recruiting for operations in Ling Chao." I stated with feigned confidence as I attempted to match his bone-crushing handshake.

"And what kind of troops did you command in the colonies, my Yankee friend?" Mr. Jacobs demanded, his nose held high in the air, an unmistakable ring of contempt in his thickly accented British voice.

"I served in command of a company of Continental Army soldiers and, after that, as the commander of a company of Vermont militiamen that was composed of both British Army deserters and allied Indians. I've been in eleven engagements, mostly against Indian hostiles but also against British regulars, loyalist militias, and the militia of the State of New York." I stated proudly, knowing that my military record was impressive.

"Very good, Mr. Lee, very good indeed. My business, one my businesses I should say, is providing mercenary troops to non-European actors. My customers include several semiautonomous kingdoms in the Royal Colony of India, a smattering of rather nasty warlords in the slant-eyed lands of the Far East, and a handful of slave traders and tribal chieftains in negroid Africa. Tell me, Mr. Lee, how did you hear of us, via word of mouth or through printed advertisement?"

"An advertisement in a French news pamphlet, Sir, a news pamphlet published in Marseilles."

"Ah, the French, proving yet again that their tongues are better at making love than at transmitting messages," Mr. Jacobs quipped through a thin-lipped smile. "Ling Chao is not a country but an opium warlord in the south of China, a rather cruel fellow who enjoys raping nearly as much as he revels pillaging. Unfortunately, my expedition to aid the extremely undeserving, but extremely wealthy, Mr. Ling departed almost a month ago. However, as you can plainly see, I am currently compiling another expedition to aid yet another of my many Oriental clients, the King of Siam, a sniveling little slant-eyed bastard who has been pestering me for troops for five years and has finally offered up enough gold to pique my interest. I am presently searching for a man of quality to lead this expedition to Siam. Though I would prefer a fellow Englishman, it would seem that all of my well-bodied countrymen are off fighting King George's never ending war in The Colonies. As such, I am offering you employment to serve as the commander of my expedition and as military liaison to that pathetic midget king of the forgotten jungle country of Siam. What think you?"

"I readily accept, Sir, but I must confess that I speak not a word of Portuguese." I responded hesitantly.

"That is irrelevant, the ship is Portuguese but little else. The majority of your company are German-speaking Swiss; all of the officers and most of the sergeants also speak English fluently. You will find that most of the rank-and-file comprehend elementary English even if they cannot speak the language; despite this bloody war our tongue continues to gain ground over bloody French as the international language of commerce. Come, we shall take my carriage to the encampment, there is no time for idling about, the expedition sets sail in one week."

As we rode through the vibrantly personable streets of Lisbon's upper class boroughs, Mr. Jacobs proudly informed me that he was one of the Portuguese capital's most powerful landowners, having opportunistically poured the bulk of his inheritance into Lisbon's reconstruction after the ruinous earthquake of 1755[7], a profitable investment that had exponentially multiplied Mr. Jacobs' net worth whilst simultaneously transforming the Englishman into an unlikely powerbroker in Portuguese politics. I sat quietly for most of the ride, listening politely as Mr. Jacobs pointed eagerly to structure after structure, edifice after edifice of his construction. This went on for nearly an hour and I was becoming quite bored and struggling valiantly to conceal my disinterest, willing my drooping eyelids to stay open when Mr. Jacobs abruptly twisted his whole body in his seat and directly faced me with his giant frame whilst tersely interjecting the terms of my contract. His offer seemed was surprisingly generous and included a handsome monthly salary and guaranteed death benefits for my family in the event of my premature termination due to a musket ball, a sword, or a native's spear. Death from disease was not covered but I was in no position to barter in my present downtrodden condition, something which I am sure Mr. Jacobs suspected. The cost of this generosity was a three year service commitment in the Kingdom of Siam, a lengthy commitment but terms that were nonetheless acceptable for I was a man without a country or a future, a man with nothing to lose. Lost in the thought and calculation, I had failed to notice the transition of the Lisbon metropolis into the rolling green hills of the Portuguese countryside. Arriving at our destination, Mr. Jacobs' servant eased our

7. Great Lisbon Earthquake of 1755: A massive
   earthquake that nearly wiped Lisbon off of the face
   of the map, so great was the destruction.

carriage off the road and into an expansive and smartly arranged military encampment where my new employer's mercenary army was garrisoned.

Upon spotting our carriage, the mercenary company's bugler blew the assembly call and the soldiers of Mr. Jacobs' troop poured out of their tents and sprinted into formation, a formation that was precisely centered in front of Mr. Jacobs' carriage and lined parallel to the dusty road that led from the encampment back to Lisbon. There were one hundred and twenty mercenaries in the company, a company which was organized into three platoons of forty men, each platoon commanded by a neatly attired and crisp appearing Lieutenant and a hard faced, battletested platoon sergeant. The mercenary troopers wore purple and white uniforms with black leather suspenders and tall round purple covers, a variation of the Portuguese Army's standard uniform that had been provided free of charge by Mr. Jacobs' close personal friend, the Marquis of Pombal[8],the year before the powerful Marquis was exiled from Lisbon by the newly crowned Portuguese Reina (queen)—Her Majesty Reina Maria I.

I nodded my head in satisfaction as I watched the company's First Sergeant inspecting his soldiers. It was immediately apparent to me that the mercenaries had been trained to the highest standards, a finely-oiled military machine. Content that his men were all present and that they were all groomed to his unwaveringly high standards, the First Sergeant spun an about-face and rendered me a crisp salute. Then in a thick German accent he called out, "First Sergeant Franz Loril report'd for duty, Sir. The men iz ready for de inspection, Sir." Mr. Jacobs nodded to the First Sergeant, glanced down at his shiny Swiss timepiece, and then scampered back into his carriage, rushing off to tend to another of his of entrepreneurial ventures. As he pulled away, Mr. Jacobs leaned out of the carriage's door and pointed his finger at me whilst sternly shouting, "have them ready for departure in one week, Captain, that is all."

8. Marquis of Pombal/Reina Maria I: Born Sebastiao de Carvalho e Melo to a minor aristocratic family, the Marquis of Pombal was the iron-fisted prime minister of Portugal from 1755-1770. Exercising near absolute power under the weak, pleasure-seeking Rei Joseph 1, the Marquis of Pombal turned Portuguese society on its head by abolishing slavery, expelling the powerful Jesuit Order, outlawing discrimination against non-Catholics, implementing economic and financial reforms including the imposition of a stringent tax code that was universally enforced on all strata of Portuguese society. These reforms enraged the Portuguese nobility who, led by the Tavora family, unsuccessfully attempted to assassinate King Joseph I in 1758. The Marquis of Pombal mercilessly prosecuted the Tavoras—rainy down fiery vengeance upon every man, woman, and child who was connected to the assassination plot. This iron-hearted retribution earned the Marquis the lifelong disdain of Reina Maria I, heir to the throne of Portugal, who upon the death of Joseph I stripped the Marquis of all of his titles and issued an edict requiring him to maintain himself no less than twenty miles from her person. The Marquis of Pombal died at his estate in Pombal, Portugal in 1782, a humbled man.

CHAPTER 10
Rounding the Cape

08 January 1780: Kasteel de Goede Hoop[9]: The torch lit dungeon starkly contrasted with the faded yellow and chalky white sun-bleached walls of the gargantuan Kasteel de Goede Hoop. First Sergeant Franz Loril stood facing the slick, cold granite walls of our prison cell while banging his calloused fists against the walls in a fit of rage, shouting guttural profanities in his native German. I sat slumped on the damp floor, having tired of standing hours ago, conversing soberly with my cadre, our morale abysmally low and sinking further by the moment. After a storm-battered voyage down the west coast of tropical Africa, the *Sao Rafael's* captain had elected to make a brief port call at the Dutch colony of Cape Town for repair of our wind-damaged masts and for resupply of our dwindling stock of scurvy-prophylactic citrus. My men were seasick, and against my better judgment, I had allowed them to venture onto shore into Cape Town for an evening of recreation and relaxation. As the old cliché goes, no act of kindness goes unpunished and my generosity that night had proven to be no exception when three of my soldiers had molested a local girl in a fit of drunkenly hedonistic debauchery. They had been arrested and shortly thereafter the *Sao Rafael* had been stormed by the local constables who had dragged us away in chains.

---

9. Kasteel de Goede Hoop: Castle of Good Hope in English. The Kasteel de Goede Hoop was constructed by the Dutch East India Company between 1666 and 1679 to protect the company's maritime waypoint at Cape Town from British aggressions. Cape Town and its fortifications were later taken by Britain, ostensibly for 'protection' from France, after the revolutionary French Republic invaded Holland in 1795.

The men and my cadre were frightened and they were looking to me for guidance. I fought to project an air of calm, hoping that my façade would disguise the fear that was tearing at my soul: fear of the hangman's noose, fear of a lengthy prison term, and fear of the prospect of the failing to satisfy the duty with which my employer had entrusted me. Doctor Lance Watkins, a bookish man whose outward demeanor concealed his formidable skill with both the pistol and the blade, sat next to the Macellaro brothers, Ara and Helio, two Lieutenants of Portuguese stock who commanded my company's first and second platoons, respectively. To my right sat Lieutenant Otto Bauer, a bear of a man of Swiss-German descent who commanded third platoon and was greatly respected by his soldiers for his extensive combat experience, experience gained in theaters of war that ranged from the hinterlands of the Balkans, to the evergreen forests of North America, to the impenetrable jungles of West Africa. Finally, there was First Sergeant Franz Loril, a man small in frame but large in heart whose aggressive predisposition was plainly apparent on both his saber-scarred face and his bullet-damaged left forearm, both wounds courtesy of a Turk whose life First Sergeant Loril had subsequently brought to its premature end during a naval battle in the Mediterranean.

"Eez horse sheet! How dee fuck you blame us for deeze rapist bastards." First Sergeant Loril chastised loudly, to no one in particular, his deep voice echoing off the dungeon's thick walls.

"Let's all keep our heads about us, First Sergeant, anger won't loosen the bolt of our cell door. I hear someone coming down the stairs, perhaps the Dutch magistrate has finally decided to grace us with his presence." I said calmly in a fatherly tone of voice.

The Dutch Magistrate wore flowing orange robes, robes which represented the Royal Dutch House of Orange, and a laughably pompous, ridiculously curled, shoulder length wig—the type of wig so very popular at the time in the pretentious courts of aristocratic Europe. Two portly Dutch soldiers, clad in the orange-and-yellow uniforms, flanked the magistrate on either side with their muskets cocked and held at the ready.

"Ont slutein de deur." The Dutch Magistrate demanded, his voice high pitched and raspy.

The obese, sloppily bearded jailer slid off his sitting stool and waddled over to our cell, unlatching the rusty lock with the most peculiar invention I had ever seen: a blocky brass cylinder that concealed a one-shot pistol whilst simultaneously functioning as a key.

"Who's in command of this criminal rabble?" The magistrate hissed, standing close enough to my person for me to hear the wheezing of his diseased lungs as he spoke, a medical condition that Dr. Watkins later informed me is known as dropsy.

"I am in command, Captain Jonathan E. Lee." I duly reported as I stood from the floor then bowed to him.

"Come with me, Captain, lock de rest van hen af." The Dutch Magistrate commanded as his frightened jailor accosted me out of the prison cell and then slammed the heavily barred door shut again, a loud screeching 'clank' ringing through the dungeon as its rusty lock married together.

The Dutch Magistrate led me out of the melancholy prison into the glowing warmth of the South African sun which made my darkness-accustomed eyes tear though inwardly I was

rejoicing at the sight of the bright noon sky.
I followed my captor into the Kasteel's main
hall then through the labyrinth of passageways
and staircases that led to his smartly
decorated working quarters which sat perched at
the pinnacle of the Kasteel's south tower. The
magistrate plopped down behind his desk, taking
a long pause to recover his breath as he used
the muscles of his chest and neck to assist his
fatigued lungs, seemingly inhaling with his
entire body as he rocked back and forth in his
seat. After several minutes of labored
respiration, the magistrate finally regained
his air and ordered the Kasteel's guards to
wait outside his chambers while I was
interrogated.

"This damned African dust has polluted my
airways, every day I curse accepting this
assignment." The magistrate hissed as he spit
great chunks of green-yellow phlegm into a
filthy handkerchief. "But I have another
question today, a question that perhaps you can
answer, a question that has perplexed me since
my university days at Oxford. Why do you
English think that you can do as you please
anywhere on the damned globe without the bother
of acknowledging the set of common human
conventions that the rest of mankind refers to
as 'laws'?" The Dutch Magistrate leaned forward
as he spoke like a sickly lion preparing to
pounce, his jugular veins bulging and pulsating
grotesquely with each heartbeat, his acne-
scarred face beet red and reddened further by a
comical mixture of air hunger and fury.

"I wouldn't know, Sir, for I am not an
Englishman. I am a proud Virginian, Sir." I
stated in the thickest colonial accent I could
muster.

"A colonial! What in god's name are you doing
here on this forsaken half of the world, good

man?" The magistrate managed to eject through his spell of coughing.

There was once a time in my life, a time of blessed innocence, when I would have preferred that a hot coal touch my lips than to suffer the shame of hearing them utter a lie—that time had long since passed and I now stood fully prepared to bend, break, crush, and destroy the truth if it was necessary to free myself and the men entrusted to my command from our Cape Town penitentiary. And lie I did…shamelessly lie…lie without remorse and I do not regret it.

"I am not permitted to speak of this, but given our present circumstances…" I stammered with feigned hesitance.

"Speak man, damn you to hell, speak!" The Dutch Magistrate wheezed as he broke into a chain of deep hacking coughs, the words exited his mucus-frothing mouth accompanied by phlegm that flew across his desk onto the freshly polished marble floor.

"Very well, Sir. You leave me no alternative but to break my sacred oath of silence and to inform you that I am the commander of a clandestine expedition, financed by the Continental Congress, to conduct raids against the British in the Indian Ocean. Our great hope is to bring the warfare of the Revolution against the weak underbelly of the bloated British Empire and thus force King George III to deploy greater numbers of his frigates away from our blockaded shores. My crew does not know our true mission and I will deny its existence to any other man to protect my beloved country. I offer my sincerest apologies for the transgressions of my mercenaries and I hope with all of my heart that you will allow me the pleasure of watching the three men who are guilty of this heinous crime swing high from the gallows. I pray that after the perpetrators of this evil rape have been punished that you will allow the remainder of my command free passage to continue our vital mission."

"I have great respect for your revolutionary cause, my Yankee friend, great respect indeed. God knows that I, and the House of Orange mind you, support your infant nation wholeheartedly." The magistrate said with openly welcoming palms, his tense body relaxing and his spell of coughing easing. "But you have put me into a difficult position, an impossibly difficult position. The citizens of Cape Town, my citizens, are craving for blood and protesting in the streets to demand it no less. Hmm…a predicament indeed, a difficult predicament with an answer that is staring me right in my face! Yes, I will have you and your men serve as the criminals' executioners! That will placate my citizens and then you can be on your way to fight the cursed British, perhaps kill some of them in my honor!"

The Dutch Magistrate rose from his chair with a gently evil grin creeping up his plethoric face, his bulbous nose even redder than usual as he strolled to the door and called for the Kasteel's servants to fetch us a pot of tea and a plate of cookies, a British custom which the magistrate explained that he had grown fond of during his four years of study at Oxford. I sipped my tea slowly, oblivious to the fact that the steaming liquid was searing my lips, trying not to think of the task that I now must perform in the morning—the execution of my own men.

09 January 1780: The condemned rapists shook with nervous tremors as they approached the hastily constructed gallows, their hands tightly bound behind them as they were led to their death at gunpoint by my cadre. I pulled

the creaking wooden handle and activated the
gallows' trap door. The rapists dropped and the
life slowly exited their bodies and they
futilely kicked in kicked about at the air.
Then they were still—dead. That is all.

10 January 1780: Resupplied generously by the
Dutch Magistrate we resumed our journey to the
Kingdom of Siam on smooth seas and powered by a
gentle eastward wind.

CHAPTER 11
Taaksin the Great

03 March 1780: After an uneventful voyage from Cape Town through the tranquil waters of the Indian Ocean the *Sao Rafael* arrived offshore the newly constructed capital of Siam, Thon Buri. Our frigate was met by the King of Siam's imperial envoy at the mouth of the Chao Phraya River, a great winding, dark-blue river that transected the center of the Siamese capital and comprised, along with an extensive system of canals, the capital city's main artery of transit. Thon Buri's architecture was so magnificently exotic that I fear paper and pen can never fully do justice to its grandeur. The banks of the Chao Phraya were lined with golden wats[10], towering government centers with intricately sculptured sandstone walls and teak wood roofs, and enormous Siamese boxing stadiums, all of these structures rising from the thick tropical foliage to tower over the tops of gently swaying rattan trees. The wat complexes were arranged in square and rectangular formations with a centrally located main temple with walls that rose in steep triangular patterns, similar to the Egyptian pyramids save with narrower bases and also differing in that they climbed upwards in a stepping pattern in place of smooth sides favored by the ancient pharaohs. A broad, central staircase lead into each temple's vast inner chambers where orange robed monks lived and performed religious ceremonies, not unlike the employment of Christian monks in the monasteries of Europe. Each wat complex—of which there were dozens located throughout Thon Buri—was meticulously gilded in glimmering gold and constructed of the highest quality sandstone, sandstone of such red, white,

10. Wat: Buddhist temple complex.

orange, and brown beauty that it rivaled the
finest marble to be found in Rome. The
government edifices were of similar
construction to the wats, though of lesser
scale and grandeur, and these buildings were
scattered throughout Thon Buri as numerously as
the red ants that crawled through the
surrounding jungles, a testament to the
preeminence of the Siamese monarch's
dictatorial regime. The city's boxing stadiums
hosted gladiatorial muay boran[11] matches, a form
of boxing that was Siam's national sport, and
they peppered the residential sectors of Thon
Buri and were surrounded by the sturdy bamboo
huts of the peasantry.

My men crowded the *Sao Rafael's* poop deck
as we filled our sea-weary eyes with Thon
Buri's alien scenery. As we stared in mystified
fascination, the king's envoy approached our
ship in their large, brown, flat-bottomed,
green-roofed river junks. The captain ordered
the cannon to fire a welcoming salute as we

11. Muay Boran: Siamese boxing, also referred to as 'the
    science of nine limbs' because its practitioners use
    punches, elbows, knee strikes, kicks, and head butts
    against their opponents (two fists, plus two feet,
    plus two knees, plus two elbows, plus one head
    equals nine). A brutal form of hand-to-hand combat,
    both in the boxing ring and on the battlefield, that
    frequently claimed the lives of its participants. In
    muay boran fights, unlike in western boxing, the
    fighters wear no gloves to cushion their blows and
    frequently wrap their hands in thick hemp ropes that
    tear open their opponent's flesh. Muay boran also
    incorporates standing grappling: throwing an
    opponent to the floor is quite legal although
    grappling on the ground is not. The lack of a ground
    grappling dimension is due to the fighting style's
    direct translation from the battlefields,
    battlefields strewn with spear-wielding soldiers
    whose presence necessitates that the only practical
    strategy for a fighter misfortunate enough to find
    himself on the ground is to stand up as quickly as
    possible.

waved to the round bamboo hat wearing, brightly robed, broadly smiling men of the Siamese envoy as they tied their river junks to the *Sao Rafael* and climbed aboard on the ropes that we tossed down to them from the decks.

The Chao Phraya was a deep river that maintained its depth as our frigate sailed cautiously inland at a painstakingly slow pace, much to the annoyance of our Siamese escorts, for the *Sao Rafael's* captain was highly afraid of running aground in the river and he insisted on continually checking our depth as our frigate inched forward down the mighty river. Shallow bottomed Siamese merchant junks passed by us—the Siamese sailors, merchants, and soldiers aboard gawking up at our deck as they sailed past. I marveled at the bustling pace of the densely trafficked river as I watched dozens of junks entering and exiting the Chao Phraya via the seemingly infinite number of canals that connected Thon Buri's outlying districts with the centrally-located river. The junks were as ubiquitous on the Chao Phraya as horses and carriages crowd the streets of Philadelphia! Lining the river banks were Siamese women and children who were bathing in the river and collecting cooking water for their daily chores in wooden buckets, all of them wearing peculiar straw hats that were reminiscent of European lamp shades.

After finally reaching the conclusion of our exhaustingly slow trek, the captain dropped anchor in front of the king's palace, a colossal conglomeration of bright yellow-orange sandstone step pyramids with loudly painted teak wood and bamboo leaf awnings overhanging board leisure decks and steep staircases that led into the palace's spacious innards. My cadre and I disembarked, bidding the captain fair well as we were led by the Siamese envoy to meet our new master, the King of Siam. I entered the king's throne room flanked by the

Siamese envoy's interpreter, who called out to
announce our presence for all to hear as he
dropped to his knees and bowed deeply to the
king, so deeply that his entire chest touched
the floor as he performed an intricate Siamese
bowing ritual that is reserved only for
royalty. My cadre and I bowed in the European
fashion, taken aback by the grandeur of the
court and hoping that our ignorance of Siamese
culture would not offend our powerful host. The
Siamese monarch, King Taaksin, sat upon a solid
gold throne that was framed in emeralds and
sapphires that shone so radiantly that they had
a blinding effect from clear across the
immense, teak-walled throne room, walls which
were decorated with life-sized engravings of
the king's martial exploits. The omnipotent
King Taaksin was a young and muscular man of
perhaps, forty years of age, with a stern yet
handsome face that projected the great man's
persona much as a telescope magnifies the
heavens, engulfing the throne room with the
aura of the king's absolute power. King Taaksin
waved my entourage forward and we cautiously
advanced towards him with our heads bowed, a
nervous lump in each officer's throat, the
nervous sweat dripping down our backs and
overpowering the best efforts of the two dozen
scantily clad women who fanned the throne room
with palm leaves of such size that I wondered
how such petit bearers could manage to hold
them. As we neared the Siamese throne, the king
suddenly leapt to his feet and flashed a
radiant smile, a smile that was so broad that
it nearly succeeded in reaching his ears.

"Sawat dee cup (hello)!" The king shouted in a
pleasantly ringing, musical tone as he raised
his hands until they were clasped, palms
together, directly in front of his face, his
thumbs pointing backwards toward his neck, his
fingers held tightly together pointing skywards
whilst the king simultaneously bowed his
crowned head and rendered the traditional

Siamese gesture of greeting. Recovering from his bow, he began to speak through the envoy's translator. "Welcome to my beautiful kingdom, I am grateful for your presence and I hope that your long journey was comfortable. The enemies of Siam surround me on all sides and my army, though valiant, is unlearned in the ways of modern warfare. My enemies—the Burmese, the Lao, and the Khmer—have stolen our sacred lands, the lands of our ancestors, and I will never rest until my people have returned to their rightful place as the rulers of the entirety the ancient Kingdom of Ayutthaya. Yet my best efforts have been frustrated by the European guns and cannon that our enemy has been taught to use in ways that are foreign to us. I have purchased these weapons, weapons that your European merchants assure me—assure me on their lives—are of greater quality then my enemy's. Yet I continue to lose three times as many men as my foes every time we cross fangs. My victories are costly and I am forced to spend far too much time raiding in the southern lands for slaves to restock my depleted ranks, time that would be better spent fighting my enemies to the east and to the west. This is why you are here, to correct this regretful imbalance."

The king gesticulated wildly as he spoke, flaying his arms about whilst pacing to-and-fro, speaking as much with his body as he did with his mouth to such an effect that the presence of our translator was almost unnecessary. I stepped forward six inches and with my head bowed as I began to speak: "Greetings my lord! My employer, Mr. Jacobs, sends his goodwill along with many crates full of gifts of English wools and Spanish silvers, as you requested during your correspondence. My men and I appear before you ready to begin our work; please show me the army that we are to train for we are eager to begin our task."

Before the words had left my mouth, King Taaksin stormed off at a furious pace, almost a trot, whilst waving his arm forward in a great circle, beckoning for us to follow him out of his throne room and through the palace's winding passageways. The king talked wildly as he cantered forth, the words spewing from his mouth too quickly for our interpreter to translate, the interpreter apologizing in exasperation whist simultaneously attempting (in vain) to paraphrase the gist of the king's endless flight of ideas. The officers and I scurried after him, our hearts pounding as we followed the king's long trail of rippling golden-orange robes, breaking into profuse full body sweats as we exited the cool palace into the unforgiving Siamese sun. The courtyard was blooming with row after row of meticulously groomed white and red petal orchids, finely pruned trees that were cloaked in snake-like vines, green and yellow bananas, low-hanging mangos, and solid brown coconuts large enough to crack a man's skull open if he were to be so unfortunate as to be standing underneath the mother tree when their fruit ripened and tumbled to the earth. The king swerved around a startled elephant, its rider sitting high atop and trying desperately to swerve the agitated beast out of our path, King Taaksin seemingly oblivious to the danger of the great beast's massive feet which came crashing down inches from my face. The king rounded a narrow, towering paisley-ornamented temple to enter the adjacent field where we were confronted by a mass of five thousand Siamese soldiers who were sitting idly on the closely trimmed grass.

"KAWT TAWT (excuse me)!" The king bellowed as he expelled the entirety of the air from his lungs.

The peasant-robed soldiers and their finely dressed officers leapt to their feet. A yellow silk-clad and spiraling gold-crowned general hurriedly climbed onto his elephant and rode over to us, dismounting and bowing deeply to his king. Confronted with his general, King Taaksin's arms flailed about even more wildly than before as his face darkening into a deep red-brown, the king shouting at the top of his lungs as he waved his spear-wielding guards towards the trembling, elderly general.

"The king is displeased," stated our interpreter in the bored monotone of a man accustomed to witnessing such violent outbursts. "The king says that he ordered for the men to stand in formation while waiting for our arrival and that he is very disappointed that he found them sitting on the grass. The general is now saying that it was extremely hot today, with much humidity, and that…"

The translator's words hung in the air as we both stared wide-eyed as the king's body guards grabbed the petrified little general and threw him to the ground, holding the terrified and protesting man in place whilst their king leapt into the air and drew his twin krabi[12], landing on his startled general beginning to hack him to death, the Siamese soldiers looking on in silence. The general's screams were deafening as King Taaksin lopped clump after clump of flesh from his target's body, hacking at his target for what seemed like a small eternity, not stopping until the king's son, a fifteen year old prince with hardened soldier's eyes, pulled his father off the profusely bleeding general and instructed the king's body guards to administer the coup-de-grace, an order which they obliged by offing the finely dressed man's screeching head onto the finely trimmed parade field. It was at that moment that my cadre and I fully appreciated the way of Siam—the way of King Taaksin.

12. Krabi: A single-edged hacking sword with a wood or ivory handle and a thin, 24 inch blade, similar in appearance to a machete. Siamese warriors typically

carried two krabi ('daab song mue') holding one in
each hand during combat. The krabi was wielded at
the enemy in hacking arcs; typically being swung
with the posterior sword-holding hand attacking
whilst the swordsman simultaneously pivots on his
front foot 180 degrees while swinging his rear leg
forward in a lunging motion so that the rear foot
and rear hand end as the soldier's front pointing
appendages. This increases the reach of the krabi
strike from 2-3 ft. to 5-6 ft. whilst simultaneously
setting the soldier up for his next strike (again
with the rear hand, which was the front hand at the
beginning of the strike). Soldiers striking in the
manner appear as if they are walking forward with
great strides while swinging their krabi in a
windmill pattern. This is the same footwork
technique that is used by Siamese boxers to throw
the devastating Siamese roundhouse kick, which is so
powerful that the heavily conditioned shin of the
leg is used to land the kick instead of the foot for
the small bones of the foot would break if it were
used to deliver the strike. Note: the deathblow from
a krabi was usually by decapitation.

Later that evening, the king offered my
officers and I luxurious accommodations
complete with servants-in-waiting and pleasure
women, generosities that I graciously refused
much to my cadre's displeasure for I am a man
of the firm conviction that officers should
live in the field with their soldiers. I set to
the task of training the king's army well
before dawn the morning of the day after our
arrival, my spirits raised high by the
difficulty of the challenge that confronted me
for I have always been a man who thrives in the
face of adversity. Indeed, in retrospect, I now
believe that my drunken escapades in Europe
were more the consequence of want of productive
employment than due to melancholy longing for
my native Virginia. The Army of the Kingdom of
Siam numbered 95,000 strong with 45,000 of
these troops distributed amongst the garrisons
that dotted the jungles of the Siamese
frontiers in all four of the cardinal
directions, garrisons which were especially
concentrated along the western borders of the
kingdom where the threat from Siam's eternal

enemy, The Kingdom of Burma, perpetually endangered the fledgling Siamese state. King Taaksin had not forgotten the merciless Burmese annihilation of the ancient Kingdom of Ayutthaya a mere forty years prior. Indeed, it was the catastrophe of that apocalyptic invasion that had destroyed the old Ayutthayan/Siamese monarchy and that had paved young Taaksin's road to power.

I learnt of the story of King Taaksin the Great the night of my arrival, told during whispered conversations by my newly assigned Siamese interpreter, a young British-educated warrior named Tuk. The son of an bankrupt Chinese merchant and his sickly Siamese wife, the future king had been born into a life of depravity, forced to spend his childhood scouring the sewers of Ayutthaya—the ancient Siamese capital city—hunting for vermin to eat until at the age of thirteen the young man was forcibly conscripted into the Ayutthayan army. In the Ayutthayan military the charismatic young Taaksin had proven himself a talented leader of soldiers, a skill that was equally matched by his cunning, his martial genius, and his unmatched physical fortitude. The future king excelled in the intricate strategies of the Siamese martial arts, both on the battlefield and in the muay boran fights that he regularly engaged in when stationed in garrison both to pass time and to earn pocket change to finance his ravenous sexual appetite. Despite the strength of Ayutthaya's martial legacy, a legacy which stretched back at least a millennium, the kingdom had degenerated into the decadence that so often grows from the wealth and luxury of success, like a Roman Empire of the Orient. As great success wrought great sloth, Ayutthaya's hardy warrior ethos degenerated into a weakly hedonism, a cancer that internally consumed the great empire and left it so weakened that when the Burmese attacked in that fateful year, 1767, the King

of Ayutthaya could find no men willing to man
the kingdom's extensive stocks of modern
European muskets, cast-iron cannon, and
sophisticated explosives. The Burmese sacked
Ayutthaya and razed its golden temples to the
ground. The conquerors marched the defeated
empire's citizens through the unforgiving
jungles of Indochina back to Burma, thousands
of Siamese dying of starvation during their
march of misery, thousands more passing from
the diseases that froth thickly through the
jungle airs. Those lucky enough to survive that
death march only found more suffering at the
end of their journey, a life of slavery in the
Kingdom of Burma.

Yet many Siamese escaped the destruction
that surrounded them, hiding in the thick
tropical forests and in the remote villages
that peppered the Siamese backcountry as
thickly as flies cover a pie that has been left
on a windowsill, villages so secluded and so
concealed by the dense jungles that no
foreigners has or likely ever will lay eyes
upon them. Taaksin was one of these fortunates
who escaped the fate of his now enslaved
countrymen. The ambitious young man sensed the
power- void that was left by the vanquished
Ayutthayan monarchy, tasted its promise, and
succeeded in uniting the scattered Siamese into
a fit of nationalistic fervor. Horrible warfare
followed as King Taaksin's rebel armies fought
to expel the Burmese from their lands.
Nauseating numbers of casualties piled high on
both sides, losses suffered gladly by the
humiliated Siamese but only reluctantly by
their Burmese conquerors, Burmese whose armies
were filled with conscripts who were fighting
far from their homes, far from their families,
and in territories that meant nothing to them.
After years of combat, years of attrition, the
tide turned in favor of the Siamese, cementing
the new king's power. King Taaksin established
a new capital city, Thon Buri, south of the

former capital of Ayutthaya, which lied in
ruins from years of Burmese cannonade and
plunder. The new king immediately set to work
replenishing the depleted population of his
kingdom via vast forced migrations[13] of both the
Siamese, the Malay, and the tribal populations
of Siam's heavily populated, but loosely
governed, southern peninsular regions,
uprooting the masses and replanting them in the
villages of the fertile plains that surrounded
the king's new capital. King Taaksin was a man
driven by a sole purpose—to exact revenge on
the hated Burmese and to restore Siam to its
former glory—an obsession that possessed the
king's every thought, his every waking moment.
The king had assembled 55,000 of his best
soldiers, all of the men that could be safely
spared from garrisons on the Burmese and
Laotian borders, to Thon Buri. It was these
men, this powerful army, that Taaksin had
tasked me with transforming into the weapon
that would finally realize his greatest
ambition—to subjugate the entirety of Indochina
under the yoke of Siam.

13. Forcible Relocation of Peasants: A common theme in
    the history of Indochina for as long as humans have
    populated that large, fertile peninsula. Though the
    rice paddies of Indochina provide a rich bounty of
    crops that are capable of feeding a dense
    population, the region's fertility is
    counterbalanced by a substantial burden of
    population-attenuating diseases, such as malaria and
    dysentery, which when coupled with the area's
    constant warfare have combined to make a shortage of
    manpower, in both the farm fields and in the
    military ranks, a source of constant worry for the
    Indochinese kings. Thus, one of the major spoils of
    war in Indochinese conflicts is the relocation of
    the defeated party's population to serve in the rice
    paddies and in the armies of the victors.

CHAPTER 12
Muay Boran

On taking command of the royal army, I found myself shocked by the primitive state of my soldiers who stood dressed in peasant's garb, albeit neatly worn peasant's garb, each man clothed in a white short-sleeved shirt that was tucked neatly into a pair of tan high-water pants, each soldier's head shaved shiny bare and covered with a broad-brimmed straw hat to protect him against that most deadly foe of the Siamese battlefield, the blistering tropical sun. My men bore traditional Siamese weapons, not a musketman to be had in the whole lot, the wealthier officers armed with either duel krabi or a single krabi and a sturdy loh[14], but the majority of the rank-and-file armed only with plong[15] and mai sun saak[16]. On the left flank there stood a stunning cavalry of one hundred oriental elephants that were decorated in wild costumes and ridden by fearsome riders who were armed with long ngao[17]. On the right flank I beheld a sight far less glamorous—several sky-stretching piles of never before touched Dutch and British muskets and a few smart, but similarly unused, cannon of French design. I had noticed that when my soldiers had been called into formation that they had given these

14. Loh: A small, round shield with a sharpened edge that is used both for deflecting blows and for slashing at the enemy.

15. Plong: Stout sticks/staffs used by the lowest rungs in the Siamese social strata as weapons of war.

16. Mai sun saak: A pair of wooden clubs strapped to a soldier's forearms, used for deflecting krabi blows and for delivering blunt strikes to the enemy.

17. Ngao: A spear weapon used by war elephant riders to impale the enemy infantry below. Note: war elephants were also used in devastating charges to trample the enemy.

modern weapons a wide berth, most of the men refusing to even look in the firearms' direction as if the weapons were a Greek Medusa. Upon inquiry, Tuk abashedly informed me that our army was composed of primitive Siamese peasants and Malay slaves and that these men were utterly terrified of the sound of musket fire, having never witnessed the action of gunpowder before a demonstration by British merchantmen two weeks prior to my arrival that had sent the panicked army fleeing en masse towards the jungle, a stampede that was only stopped by brutal reprisals from by the elephant cavalrymen. Rumor had spread through the army like a plague of the pox that the European muskets were possessed by evil spirits; thus the men stayed as far from these weapons as possible.

Sighing in exasperation, my first order of action was to divide the jumbled ranks into manageable divisions. Taking personal command of the 5,000 man strong, elite 'Tiger Guard,' with First Sergeant Loril serving as my executive officer, I apportioned the remaining 45,000 men into three divisions of 15,000 men apiece. I attached one platoon from my mercenary company, to include the platoon's cadre, to each division with Lieutenant Ara Macellaro of first platoon taking command of Division 'A', his brother Lieutenant Helio Macellaro of second platoon taking charge of Division 'B', and Division 'C' falling under the reigns Lieutenant Otto Bauer. Putting this plan into action, a rather monumental task given the wholly disorganized state of the army, an army which at that point I could only describe as a loosely aligned rabble, consumed the better portion of the day. As the sun began to set, I was all too willing to accept Tuk's suggestion that we retire to an eating establishment of his frequent patronage. The officers, First Sergeant Loril, and I followed Tuk off of the parade grounds and then out of the surrounding imperial district and into the refuse strewn backstreets of Thon Buri's vulgar underbelly, finally arriving at—much to my astonishment—one of the city's many boxing stadiums.

"What in god's name is this, man?" I asked incredulously, staring openmouthed at the boxing ring, which was discolored with stains of dried blood.

"A welcoming party, Siamese style! A night of tasty food and good boxing!" Replied Tuk as he flashed his infectious smile. "This is our national sport, muay boran, and it is the pride of my people. Please, let us find our reservation, tonight's sporting will soon begin!"

The boxing ring was a square raised platform constructed of solid teakwood planks, one tall teakwood pole standing at each of the ring's four corners and thick hemp rope wrapped around the supporting poles to enclose the ring. The floor of the ring was hard and covered in dirt—not matted like in the boxing rings in America and Europe. Tables were strewn around the ring in no particular order and scantily clad waitresses, many of them topless with their bare mammaries—voluptuous and enticing mammaries—mammaries exposed for all to see as they worked the crowd furiously selling spicy food and surprisingly good beer. The beer was warmer than I was accustomed to but exquisitely satisfying to palate of a weary soldier nonetheless.

"I suggest trying the chicken pad but I must warn you that it is quite spicy." Tuk offered while waving over a waitress in the Siamese fashion, his hand held high in a closed fist, the European raised palm gesture being considered offensive in Siam.

"I'm sure it will be lovely, Tuk, I've been dining on mariner's rations for months." I said with my mouth watering, the smells of exotic foods wafting through the air around us. "Are those the fighters, those beastly appearing fellows with the tattoos?" I inquired as my eyes continued to feast on the foreign scene that was unfolding before me. "What are is that they're putting on their hands?"

"Yes, they are the warriors and they are wrapping their hands in hemp rope to cut their opponent when they punch. It is also useful for bloodying knee and elbow strikes while defending against them." Tuk responded excitedly, clearly at home in this environment. Tuk had been a practitioner of muay boran in his youth with a renowned reputation. "Sometimes, but only in the far reaches of the kingdom now, the warriors embed the rope with broken glass to enhance the cutting effect. But alas, the king has outlawed this in Thon Buri. King Taaksin was badly cut in a fight during his youth and he bears a great scar across his chest from it. The king is never seen topless because of the shame that this scar brings to him. The ban is a decision that is not popular with the fight managers, but they are afraid of King Taaksin and dare not disobey his edict."

The Siamese cuisine proved delicious but I was soon distracted from its mouth-watering tastes by a loudly screaming Siamese announcer who was dressed in brilliantly distasteful orange, yellow, and red silk robes and a comically large, feathered headdress that sat upon his head. He leapt into the ring and the chattering patrons shifted in their seats, falling silent with anticipation. The brightly dressed and impatiently animated announcer lunged toward the left corner of the ring and pointed, with his whole body, towards the fighters as they climbed through the ropes. The hummingbird-like announcer loudly boasted each warrior's fighting record as the crowd erupted into an ear-shattering roar.

"He is announcing Doi Inthanon—it means 'the mountain' in my language—this stadium's current champion. With the blessing of the king, I arranged for Doi Inthanon to perform during tonight's fights, to perform in your honor! Doi Inthanon has fought one hundred and thirty men and he has never been defeated! He is the pride of Siam, King Taaksin's favorite fighter, and tonight he fights for you!" Tuk informed giddily.

"One hundred and thirty fights! My god man, how old is he, he looks all of twenty!" I exclaimed with a healthy dose of skepticism.

"Twenty-two years of age, barely twenty-two years of age. Doi Inthanon started fighting when he was only eight years old, that's the age when most of the champions first step into the ring, competing against other children until they are fifteen years old before graduating into the adult circuits," Tuk explained through proudly beaming eyes.

I was entranced by the appearance of this Siamese gladiator, Doi Inthanon, and I staring wide-eyed at him as he began his traditional pre-fight 'wai kru' dance[18]. The Siamese fighter lifted his muscular legs high to his front and then rotated them to the side so that his knees nearly touched his trauma-deformed ears as he pranced around the ring, stopping at each of the four corners to drop to his knees and bow so low that his chest and forehead kissed filthy floor. I was shocked by how thin, yet

18. Wai Kru: The traditional muay boran prefight ritual is performed for three reasons: 1. to honor the fighter's ancestors, 2. to ask the spirits of these ancestors for protection during the boxing match, 3. to honor Siam's greatest hero, Nai Khanom Tom. Nai Khanom Tom was a man of peasant birth who was taken

captive by the Burmese during a raid of Ayutthaya's
hinterlands many hundreds of years ago. The day of
his arrival in Burma, the Burmese king was struck
with boredom and he decided to have Burma's most
skillful boxer kill some of his newly acquired
Siamese slaves to liven up a dull afternoon. The
Burmese monarch had a boxing ring constructed in
front of his throne. Nai Khanom Tom, a practitioner
of muay boran, was the first Siamese slave selected
to fight. As the valiant peasant was led to his
execution in the ring, he performed the ceremonial
wai kru, dancing about the boxing ring and refusing
to answer his opponent's punches until his dance was
completed. After his final wai kru bow, Nai Khanom
Tom charged the Burmese boxer and split his skull
open with a powerful flying knee strike. The Burmese
king was outraged and he ordered Nai Khanom Tom to
fight nine more of Burma's most skillful boxers, all
of whom Nai Khanom Tom defeated handily and without
any rest between his fights. As his tenth fighter
fell to the floor, the King of Burma stood from his
throne and proclaimed Nai Khanom Tom a free man,
offering the Siamese peasant the choice of either a
chest of gold or two beautiful wives as his reward.
Nai Khanom Tom chose the two wives, stating that
women were harder to acquire than gold, and he then
returned to Ayutthaya where he led a simple life
farming and teaching muay boran while raising many
children.

how brawny, a physique the fighter commanded.
His abdominal muscles were grooved like a
washboard and his legs were as large as cannon,
legs that were veneered with great callouses on
the shins—the result of landing thousands of
punishing roundhouse kicks on his opponents and
of blocking the thousands of kicks that had
been thrown back at him in return. Doi
Inthanon's face was war-ravaged, his nose
flattened and his ears shriveled like
cauliflower, ears whose anatomy had been
shriveled by the friction of hundreds of
clinches—a phase of Siamese boxing combat where
the fighters grab ahold of one another whilst
landing skull-shattering elbows and rib-
fracturing knees at pointblank range. His wai
kru now completed, Doi Inthanon retired to his
corner and leaned against the ropes with a
wickedly-toothy smile of anticipation as his

opponent, Garuda, a baby-faced adolescent of only seventeen years, entered the ring and began his wai kru. The ceremonies now at an end, the two combatants leapt off of the ropes and into the middle of the ring, trading low roundhouse kicks which contacted with such force that their low-pitched thuds echoed through the stadium as the fighter's leather-rock shins walloped against one another like two boulders crashing as they rolled down a rocky hillside. The fighter's didn't bob-and-weave like western boxers, instead standing squarely upright and landing stiff jab-cross punches that were invariably either preceded or followed by a powerful roundhouse or front kick. I soon appreciated why the muay combatants stood so straight upright for the fighters next began throwing hard slicing elbows and viscerally jarring knees, knees that would surely knock the life out of a man were he to attempt to dodge his opponent by ducking downward in the fashion of European pugilism.

After lashing out with a particularly powerful flying knee that was landed on Garuda's now purple-lumped face, Doi Inthanon grabbed his young opponent and held him so closely that the two fighters' muscular chests grated against one another. The blood- sweated men clinched while exchanging a rapid staccato of knife-cutting elbows and chest-heaving knees that sent sanguine fluid flying over the amused crowd. Garuda weakened, his vision now compromised by the large gashes that stood both above and below both of his swollen eyes, losing his balance as Doi Inthanon finished him off with an uppercut elbow to the chin that cut straight down to the bone and sent a stream of blood flying onto the parasol that was drooping my table top.

"The umbrella is not only for shade!" Tuk shouted above the ear-shattering roar of the

spectators as he leaned over to collect his
betting money.

"Do all of the men in the army know how to
fight like this?" I asked hopefully, the cogs
in my head turning fast, thinking that
perhaps my army was not as ill-prepared for
combat as I had been led to believe.

"Yes, yes. Muay boran is standard military
training in Siam." Tuk explained as he raised
his forearms above the table to reveal the
knotted bone-callouses of a man who had
participated in many a muay fight.

        I had trouble sleeping that night, though
my bed was as comfortable as any to be found
either in Europe or in Virginia, a bed that had
been moved into my field tent per King
Taaksin's orders during my absence and which,
though I had planned on sleeping on the ground
like my soldiers, I thought it best not to
refuse for fear of appearing impolite to my
labile host. My thoughts were preoccupied with
the formidable hand-to-hand combat skills of my
new army. And yet, I also perseverated over
their utter lack of training with the musket,
that modern necessity of distance warfare, my
mood rapidly shifting between enthusiasm and
despair. And then it hit me—epiphany! My
mission was not to make the Siamese soldiers
into European musketmen, but rather to make
musketry Siamese. With their a priori hand-to-
hand combat skills, I stood confident that my
men had only to become moderately sufficient in
the art marksmanship to become an unrivaled
force of destruction. No, sleep would not come
to me this night, my mind spinning violently
with visions of commanding an impregnable
force, of commanding an army from hell that I
would swing as my hammer upon the enemies who
dared to impede my new master in his quest to
yoke the Orient under the iron fist of Siam!

CHAPTER 13
The Emerald Buddha

June 1780: In a country with only two seasons, rainy and dry, the rainy season arrived early in Siam and brought with its showering clouds a fog of unwelcome uncertainty that had descended upon the royal palace, a dreary fog incited by the king's descent into a great fit of melancholy. In his abysmal sadness, the king attempted to hurl himself off of the palace roof only to be, by the Grace of God, stopped at the very last moment by his loyal praetorians who escorted their master to his chambers where the great man had been shuttered away in solitude for over a month. The panicky and downtrodden atmosphere of the royal court suddenly lifted when the king unexpectedly stormed out of his self-proclaimed exile and returned to his throne in unusually high spirits, the king possessed by a seemingly endless burst of energy, an energy so powerful that the great man required only three hours of rest per night—when he slept at all. Upon my master's return, I was immediately beckoned to his throne room where King Taaksin peppered me with questions about the readiness of the army, invariably asking a second question before I had finished answering the first, an annoying habit that I had long since grown accustomed to and was, in fact, pleased to see return as the waning of this eccentricity a month prior had been a harbinger of the king's descent into his fit of melancholy.

"I have been very unhappy as of late," The king shouted through his trembling translator, "unhappy that I have failed to conquer the ancient lands of Ayutthaya, unhappy that I have yet to return my people to their righteous place of glory! No matter, I NOW HAVE AN ARMY THAT WILL BRING DEFEAT TO MY ENEMIES AND I WILL

STRIKE THEM DOWN AS THEY STRUCK DOWN MY
ANCESTORS!"

"I am proud to serve you, Your Majesty!" I
stated exuberantly, bowing to the ground as I
addressed the Siamese monarch. "The army awaits
your orders and it stands ready to execute
them!"

"Yes, you are ready, Captain Lee…no, General
Lee! You will lead my army into the pathetic
Laotian fiefdom and capture their treacherous
prince, that cowardly usurper! You will burn
his city to the ground and then you will bring
him before me to tremble before my throne!"

I had not exaggerated my army's state-of-
readiness, and less than twenty-four hours
after King Taaksin had issued his royal edict
my legions stood prepared to march. Led by nine
orange-robed Theravada Buddhist[19] monks, monks

19. Theravada Buddhism: The state religion of Siam and
most of Indochina including Cambodia, Laos, and
Burma. Theravada Buddhists follow the teachings of
Gotama Siddartha—The Buddha—a holy man who lived in
Nepal and India approximately five hundred years
before the birth of Our Savior. Buddhists believe
that existence equals suffering, that suffering is
caused by desire, and that the elimination of desire
leads to a state of harmony referred to as
'nibbana.' Buddhists believe that there are two
extremes that must be avoided in order to live a
content life: extremes of indulgence and extremes of
austerity. Buddhists show devotion to their religion
by committing themselves to a quest for personal
nibbana, by living their lives in accordance with
the example set by the Buddha, and by donating alms
to Buddhist monks. These monks are totally reliant
on this charity for sustenance for they are not
allowed to work, their only profession being to
emulate the life of The Buddha. In Indochina, the
Indian Buddhist traditions have merged with a more
ancient religion, animism, a belief that all objects
have living souls. This chimera of religions is
evidenced in Siam by the ubiquitous presence of
'spirit houses' outside of all public buildings, the
function of which is to placate any evil spirits
that might wish to cause the building's occupants
harm.

solemnly humming mantras in accordance with the
Siamese tradition, I led my army through the
cheering streets of Thon Buri with my Siamese
co-commander, General Thong Duang, stuck close
to my side. Thong Duang was a stoic and
hardnosed soldier, a childhood friend of the
king who had risen to power at Taaksin's side.
Thong Duang had led several brilliantly fought
border defenses against the hated Burmese,
battles in which the general's military genius
had singularly transformed certain defeats into
palatable stalemates. These draws against
superior Burmese forces had been hailed as
victories in the fledgling Siamese kingdom, a
kingdom whose prospects of survival had, at the
time, been tenuous at best.

As my army marched out of Thon Buri, the
peasants and their children poured onto the
streets. There were thousands of cheering
Siamese flying tiger and dragon kites whilst
screaming exuberant cheers to my soldiers as my
army filed past them in a tightly-dressed
marching formation. We exited the city and
continued our march onto the dirt roads that
wound their way through sparsely populated
country hamlets and then, when the roads ended,
trudged across the sun-scorched plains of
waist- high, razor-sharp elephant grass.
Finally, we hacked our way through tangled
jungles, jungles that my men cut our path
through with brisk machete swipes that were
fueled by nationalistic vigor. Our feet sore
and blistering but our spirits still soaring
high, my army trekked across the sediment-
filled, meandering Mekong River into Laos.

The Laotian people had long served as
vassals of the Kingdom of Ayutthaya and the
ancestral roots of the two peoples converged
upon a common history, a time when the ancient
Tai[20] people had fled southward from oppression
at the hands of the Chinese into the
Indochinese peninsula. This ancient genealogic

connection was still evident in the two peoples' shared tongue for Siamese and Laotian remained mutually intelligible dialects of the ancient common language. The Laotian capital of Wiang-chan[21]—Wiang-jun in the Laotian—was a small but densely populated and lavishly ornamented city which abutted a great bend in the Mekong. To the north, the south, and the west the city was surrounded by the river — to the east it was bordered by crowded rice paddies, rice paddies that soon transitioned into darkly chattering jungles.

I positioned my Siamese army into a semicircular formation about Wiang-chan's eastern flank, trapping the startled Lao denizens inside their city walls as the Laotian garrison's call-to-arms rang through the air and the peasantry sprinted from the rice paddies through the city's iron gates. The Laotians' surprise was complete, due in no small part to the clever politicking of my Siamese counterpart, General Thong Duang, who had used nationalistic zeal, along with bribes of gold and promises of slaves, to purchase the alliance of the western Lao—the Lao Phuan—against their eastern, Lao Wiang, brethren. General Thong Duang had informed me that the

20. Tai: An alternative spelling of the word 'Thai' that is used primarily to refer to the ancient, historical Tai people who migrated from China to the Indochina peninsula to escape Chinese persecution. The Tai included the ancestors of the current Thai, also known as the Siamese, and the Lao peoples. It should be noted that the word 'Siamese' is a European construct. The Siamese refer to themselves as 'Thai', which means 'free' in their tongue. Indeed, the average Thai would not know what a 'Siamese' is.

21. Wiang-chan: Literally, 'City of Sandalwood.' Named after a rare species of tree that is valued for its heavy, durable, and pleasant smelling wood. Wiang-chan, or Wiang-jun in Lao, is often referred to by Europeans as 'Vientiane.'

Lao Phuan, a people who lived in the amorphous border region between Laos and the Kingdom of Siam, were culturally more similar to the Siamese than to the ruling Lao Wiang, a happy fact that nicely complemented the Lao Phuan's jealously of the disproportionate power of the Lao Wiang ruling dynasty in their shared country. Thong Duang's emissaries had taken full advantage of this fraternal conflict to recruit a Lao Phuan militia to our cause. The Lao Phuan militia now stood guard on the western bank of the Mekong, across from the besieged Lao capital, blocking any possibility of a Lao Wiang retreat across the river.

The battle about to commence, I personally took command of both the Royal Tigers and of Division 'A', with both formations standing ready to attack from atop the hills that overshadowed Wiang-chan's northeastern reaches. Thong Duang took charge of Division 'B', which I positioned on our western flank, whilst First Sergeant Loril commanded Division 'C', which I had positioned to the south of the Laotian capital. I arranged our artillery battery of ten sturdy French cannon along the northern hilltops and I watched with great satisfaction as my Siamese gunners rained hellfire down upon the defenseless Lao, my artillery commander taking care to avoid the historically and religiously important Haw Phra Kew[22] temple and the Pha That Luan[23] stupa, per my explicit instructions.

22. Haw Phra Kaew: The Temple of the Emerald Buddha (in Wiang-chan, the Laotian capital).

23. Pha That Luang: A historic stupa—a stupa being a type of Buddhist temple—in Laos. According to Buddhist tradition, ten original stupas were constructed upon the death of the Buddha (circa B.C. 560 to B.C. 480), eight to house the religious patriarch's ashes, one to house the embers from his funeral pyre, and one to house his urn. Though many more stupas have been built since—on the order of

hundreds—the Pha That Luang is the most famous stupa
in Indochina.

Perched on the highest hilltop and peering
through my looking glass, I observed the
Laotian army swarming about as ants flee a
tormenting child with a pitcher of water.
Though the bulk of the Royal Laotian Army was
stricken with panic, I noticed a center of calm
in the far eastern corner of Wiang-chan, where
a collection of soldiers was assuming a
formation under the direction of an
energetically gesticulating commander whom I
assumed, correctly it turned out, to be Prince
Siribunyasen, the illegitimate monarch of the
breakaway, self-proclaimed, Kingdom of Laos. A
return to order slowly rippled through the city
as the Lao recovered from the initial shock of
my lightning assault. I silenced my cannon and
ordered my bugler to ready his instrument. As
the report of our last artillery round faded
into the distance, I instructed my bugler to
blow the call to order the infantry to commence
their assault, an order that was obeyed
immediately by my eager divisions who began
their well-choreographed march towards Wiang-
chan's steep ramparts. My men advanced not
towards the city gates, where the Lao stood
waiting with bubbling pots of searing grease
ready to be poured onto their heads, but rather
to a lightly defended section of the ramparts,
approximately one hundred meters to the south
of the city wall's main gate. Through my
looking glass I could see the confusion of the
Lao commanders, unsure of how to respond,
undoubtedly fearful of redeploying their well-
positioned forces, anticipating a strategic
feint. A devious smile crept across my sunburnt
face as my bugler blew three long toots of his
horn, a deathly music that would soon alleviate

my enemy's confusion and plainly reveal my battle plan for all to see!

As the bugler's last note faded into the wind, a great explosion rocked the city, courtesy of my advance party of Royal Tigers who had disguised themselves as Lao peasants and infiltrated Wiang-chan by digging a tunnel under a neglected section of the city wall and planting explosives, explosives which had now been ignited into a fiery explosion that blew a gaping hole into what had only moments before been an impregnable fortification. The men of Divisions 'B' and 'C' broke their ranks and rushed forward through the breach, most of the men not bothering to discharge their muskets, preferring instead to hack the horrified Lao defenders with blows from their crudely sharpened and oft splintering krabi. I held Division 'A' in reserve, the men of the division loudly protesting to join the fight, a request which I, now seeing that there was no danger of a Lao counterattack, grudgingly acquiesced to for fear of mutiny if I held back my blood thirsty soldier's for a moment longer. The battle was decided in under an hour, the Lao monarch—Prince Siribunyasen—shackled in heavy Siamese chains, the Kingdom of Laos no more, the province now returned to its rightful place as a province of Siam!

After confirming the identity of the captured prince with the aid of my Lao Phuan allies, First Sergeant, General Thong Duang, and I toured the carcass strewn Lao capital, my Royal Tigers accompanying us to protect our entourage from the looting Lao Phuan militiamen and from the soldiers of my own army, who were already freely imbibing in Wiang-chan's ample supplies liquor. General Thong Duang offered me a celebratory swig of this famous brew, which he referred to as Mekong Whiskey—though I found its taste more akin to that of the Caribbean rum that I had freely partaken with Captain

Rafael during my voyage from America to Europe
than to any whiskey of European or Colonial
distillation. General Thong Duang led us
through the defeated city, a sadistic smile
lighting across his face as he intentionally
stepped on the bodies of every dying Lao
soldier who was unfortunate enough to find
himself lying in our path. The Siamese general
led us to the Haw Phra Kaew Temple, much to my
disappointment for I desired very much to
explore the grandeur of the more famous Pha
That Luang stupa, that pride of Laos that lies
in the center of Wiang-chan. Nonetheless, I
followed the eager general through the eerie
streets and we soon found ourselves standing in
front of the the Haw Phra Kaew, a modest red
pagoda with a pointy golden roof and a grey
stone base that was surrounded by a small
orange fence. We climbed the temple's
staircase, a narrow stone incline that led into
the main chambers. As our party was preparing
to penetrate into the temple's innards, Thong
Duang tersely commanded that First Sergeant
Loril and I remove our boots. I diplomatically
protested, attempting to explain to my Siamese
counterpart that our feet were swollen and
suffering from the rotting effects of the
jungles, jungles so damp that they compelled a
man to change his socks several times a day to
keep his feet from rotting off clear off of his
body. Yet the general would not budge, blocking
our path until First Sergeant and I grudgingly
complied and removed our sweaty footwear, both
of us too tired from the day's battle to
attempt a reasoned argument with a savage. Our
boots now removed, we entered the main
chambers, pitch black save for at the far wall,
where in the torchlight we beheld an exotic
green statue that was known to the Siamese as
the Emerald Buddha[24]. The statue rested on a
solid gold, bejeweled throne, its body dressed
in the finest of silks and its head topped with
a crown that was studded with exotic jewels.
Thong Duang burst into a sprint and grabbed the

statue off of its throne, holding it high above his head whilst letting loose an animalistic cry as he ran out of the temple, stopping on the steps and shouting to the Royal Tigers who stood guard below, "we have it, we have recaptured the Emerald Buddha and we will not rest until it has been returned to its sacred throne in the land of our ancestors! Nothing can stop us now!"

A week after the fall of Wiang-chan, an ornately robed messenger arrived on elephant-back from Thon Buri and delivered a parchment that reiterated the king's orders to burn the enemy city. Additionally, the king instructed General Thong Duang and I to garrison the captured Laotian territory with one Siamese division while using the remainder of our army to forcibly relocate 30,000 Lao Wiang to the lands surrounding Thon Buri to help replenish the populations of the outlying Siamese villages that were still reeling from the aftermath of the long, destructive wars with Burma. These terrible wars, wars that had seen

24. Emerald Buddha: An 18 inch tall statue, actually constructed of green jasper (not emerald), that according to Buddhist legend was sculpted by a famous monk, Nagasena, in his homeland of India. Siamese tradition holds that the Emerald Buddha was sent to Ceylon for protection during a period of Indian civil war and that this is where the statue remained until the King of Burma, a new convert to Buddhism, requested that the Ceylonese send the holy relic to his kingdom to aid him in convincing his animistic subjects to convert. The ship carrying the relic was blown off course, landing in Cambodia instead of Burma, where the Emerald Buddha resided under the auspices of the Khmer kings until the fall of Angkor Wat to the Ayutthayan Siamese in 1432. The Ayutthayan's commandeered the Emerald Buddha as a spoil of war and took it to their northern city of Chiang Mai. A Lao prince, Lao Xang, sacked Chiang Mai in 1552 and took the statue with him back to Laos, placing it in the Haw Phra Kaew temple where it resided in great honor until recaptured by Siam during King Taaksin's invasion in 1780.

tens of thousands of civilian deaths and
another 60,000 Siamese carted off to Burma in
captivity, a hemorrhaging of population that
continued to depress rice yields in Siam, rice
that was needed to feed the king's hungry
armies.

   Though I had grown fond of Wiang-chan, for
it was a quaint little city with a plethora of
pleasantly exotic Lao traditions and cultural
nuances, I followed my orders, mostly anyhow,
and I lit Wiang-chan ablaze save for the Pha
That Luang and Haw Phra Kaew, which I could not
bring my heart to destroy, a sentiment with
which even the stone-hearted General Thong
Duang, who was busy at work wresting the
defenseless Lao Wiang peasants from their huts,
agreed. Leaving Division 'C' under the command
of First Sergeant Loril and Lieutenant Otto
Bauer, with instructions to maintain control of
the captured Laotian territory and to cement
the tributary relationship of the new Lao
puppet government with its masters in Siam,
General Thong Duang and I marched our
victorious army back across the Mekong River
and began our march home to Thon Buri. At the
head of our army the most respected, and the
most ferocious, of the elite Royal Tigers
carried the Emerald Buddha on its golden
throne, our nine rhythmically chanting monks
marching behind the holy statue of in
accordance with the traditions of the land.

CHAPTER 14
The Rise of Thong Duang

April 1782: The flames sweeping through the Khmer capital, Oudang, burnt so brightly that they illuminated the night sky and permitted me to write to King Taaksin to inform him of the success of our latest conquest without the aid of torchlight. Prince Ang Eng, the four year old Khmer monarch, wept into his pillow, his nanny too shaken to offer the child any comfort. I allowed the pitiful duo to share my personal tent under the watchful guard of two of my most loyal Royal Tigers for I felt great remorse that the boy had been present when we had slain his regent, the treacherous Prince Talaha, a man responsible for great atrocities against the Siamese during their years of weakness after the Burmese invasions. My Royal Tigers had decapitated the squirming rat, Prince Talaha, on his throne as King Taaksin had explicitly commanded, the boy-king standing only feet away from the gory spectacle.

Over the past eighteen months I had grown close to Taaksin, spending much of my time with the Siamese monarch whenever I found myself back in Thon Buri during the lulls in my military campaigning, time I had initially spent with the king out of diplomatic prudence but later shared with him because Taaksin and I sincerely enjoyed one another's company. I taught the Oriental monarch to play chess and, much to my annoyance, he rapidly surpassed my skill in this most European of all games. Indeed, the king was far from the savage I had initially taken him for in my prejudicial ignorance; I had rapidly grown to admire his undeniable genius, an admiration that was only compounded when I personally witnessed the busy king learn the English language in just two months' time, an accomplishment that had served to further cement our relationship since we could now converse without the aid of a translator. But Taaksin's charismatic personality masked a deeply troubling darkness: the king was an unrepentant slaughterer of all who dared to oppose him, even those of noble birth, a nobility that had long enjoyed a life of impunity under the elitist Ayutthayan dynasties and that now quivered in fear at the sight of their dictatorial monarch. The aristocrats were bent under the king's iron grip and any perceived treachery by the nobles was punished with the same draconian brutality that befell criminals from the peasant and mercantile classes. King Taaksin's hold on Siam grew tighter by the day as the king forcibly relocated thousands-upon-thousands of Siamese from their homes in the hinterlands closer to the villages of the fertile Chao Phraya plain that surrounded the Thon Buri, the king preoccupied with increasing rice production to feed the ever swelling ranks of his armies.

Yet this powerful man's absolute control of his country did not extend to control over himself, a weakness that became all the more apparent as I grew closer to my friend and employer. King Taaksin frequently fell into the depths of melancholy, paralyzing the government for weeks at a time as he sulked about his chambers in strict solitude, muttering to himself, only to invariably emerge from his self-imposed exile in a flurry of unnaturally high spirits with grandiose plans for his next destructive conquest. The king's ambitions seemed to have no bounds, the king willing to pay any price in the blood of his soldiers and willing to suffer any hardship upon his people to accomplish his unrelenting quest to dominate Indochina.

Taaksin's brazen ruthlessness was matched by only one other in the kingdom: Taaksin's boyhood friend, General Thong Duang, who was busily employed slaughtering the remnants of the Burmese occupation force in the desolate frontiers that surrounded the northern city of Chiang Mai. Chang Mai had once been a great metropolis but had been reduced to a mere village during the Burmese Wars with its population now further depleted by the king's forced migrations to his rapidly expanding capital city. Essentially ruling as a regent in the north, indeed throughout the entire kingdom during Taaksin's incapacitating bouts of self-isolation, Thong Duang was a shrewd self-promoter who, unlike the king, took great care to balance his dictatorial commands with popular building projects such as his patronage of elaborately constructed temples and modern boxing stadiums that were now to be found in every major city and town in the kingdom, even in the Laotian vassal. General Thong Duang was especially admired by the army due to his frequent proclamations of weeks of rest-and-relaxation for the rank-and-file between war campaigns, a welcome change of pace for soldiers who were accustomed to working seven days per week without rest. The general's lax enforcement of the laws with regards to the nobility made him similarly popular with the aristocracy, an aristocracy that grew to resent Taaksin's heavy-handed rule more and more every passing day. I noticed that King Taaksin seemed oblivious to his general's poorly disguised ambitions, perhaps, I thought, because the king relied so heavily on the Thong Duang during his bouts of mental infirmity or, perhaps, because the two men had been so close during their childhood and during their synergistic rise to power. Unlike my friend the king, I personally viewed Thong Duang with a healthy dose of cautious suspicion. Despite my best efforts to conceal this prejudice, I had no illusions that the clever general was cognizant of my true inclinations towards him.

Returning from my thoughts, I picked up my pen and completed my report to King Taaksin, jotting a friendly challenge to a game of chess at the bottom of the parchment. Sweltering in the Khmer heat, I was just about drop my quill when I heard the great rumbling commotion of an elephant parading up to my command tent. I had risen from my stool and opened my tent's drapes to find myself facing a harried appearing messenger, sweat dropping from his brow, his gaze directed at the ground as he handed me a tightly wrapped scroll that was waxed shut with the royal emblem. I called Tuk to translate the message while thinking to myself that it was odd that I should require Tuk's services for Taaksin had long since taken to the habit of writing to me in English. Tuk shuddered nervously as he read the scroll aloud, choking on his words whilst fighting back tears.

General Lee,

I regret to inform you of an unfortunate happening. Taaksin has descended into the depths of madness and I, as head of the royal garrison of Thon Buri, have been forced to relive our former leader of his official duties and to assume the powers of the throne for the welfare of our sacred people. General Lee, you are ordered to garrison your army in the Khmer territory and to return, with all of your European officers, to Thon Buri immediately for further instruction.

I eagerly await your arrival, do not delay, King Phyra San, 1st

My heart sunk into the pit of my queasy gut, like a stone tossed into a stormy sea, as I rushed to convene an emergency council of my cadre, men whom I found to be substantially less concerned about the fate of our employer than was I, undoubtedly because they lacked, and perhaps even quietly disdained, the personal bonds that I had cultivated with him.

"Perhaps it is for the best," Lieutenant Helio Marcellaro said in a reserved optimism, "Taaksin has been acting very strangely and our contract is nearly complete; thank the Lord in Heaven."

"I agree wit dis! Who give a fuck if de slant eyes wish to get rid of dis crazy bastard!" Mumbled First Sergeant Loril, the smell of Mekong whiskey thick on his breath as it had been every time we had spoken since the Laotian campaign. "One Orient' king is de same as de next." He exclaimed, gesturing upwards with his palms in an exaggerated expression of indifference.

"But the king, King Taaksin, is our employer, the man who pays our wages and puts the food in our bellies!" I shouted, scanning the room for nods of agreement and finding none. "We have an army capable of reconquering Thon Buri, do we not owe it to Taaksin to rescue him from these treacherous mutineers!"

"My alliance iz to Mr. Jacobs an' de company, not dis Siamese, dis Taaksin." First Sergeant Loril blurted out as he took another swig of whiskey, not bothering to conceal his flask. "I know dat Lieutenant Bauer wud agree, wud agree if he had not die in de latest Burma war. We haz already lost one of us and who even know how many of de soldiers we now missing. We should dank God we iz alive and go home now!"

"If I might be so bold, Jonathan, the readiness of the army is abysmal no thanks to a plague of cholera that is spreading like a brushfire through the ranks, ranks that are still suffering from the effects of the blight of typhus that is only now beginning to remit." Said Dr. Watkins in a professional monotone. "I estimate our fighting strength at no greater than fifty percent, probably less if we embark on another forced march through the jungles to reach Thon Buri."

With downcast eyes and exhaling in exasperation, I conceded defeat. "Very well, I will not force an unwelcome war upon you, not when we are so very close to completing our deployment, though my heart burns to march on Thon Buri and to punish those responsible for this wicked cabal. I have grown fond of this country, too fond, and I must not let my personal affections for the king cloud my judgment. Assemble our mercenaries and order the Siamese divisions to stand fast until orders are received from Thon Buri. It is imperative that we keep word of the king's plight from reaching the ears of the Siamese rank-and-file. Tuk, you will guard the messengers who brought us this cursed news and keep them out of earshot of the formations. If any of the messengers suffers a loose tongue, kill him. The Macellaro brothers will assist you in this task. Is that understood?"

An enthusiastic, "understood, Sir", erupted from my cadre as a less than motivated Tuk stated, "I will perform my duty, General Lee," addressing me by my Siamese rank rather than my mercenary company rank.

Much to my relief, the cadre and I managed to assemble our mercenary troop and to sneak away in the night without alerting our Siamese soldiers. How very fitting that the Oriental monsoons had begun the day after we commenced our dreary retreat to Thon Buri, I thought, as bullets of rain poured down upon my head with the force of flying locusts splattering against a window. The rain only paused for long enough to allow the mid-day sun a chance to beckon the swarms of tenacious mosquitoes out of the jungle brush, mosquitoes that pecked at our sun-blistered skin and left it raw and inviting to that other great scourge of Siam, the insatiable land leech, which feeds by crawling up a man's trousers, gently biting so as not to be noticed by its unfortunate host, sucking blood until it is as round as a Cuban cigar. Trudging through the mud, I halted my company only long enough for the men to take a brief nap and to clean the caked sludge from their musket barrels. Then we marched again, fighting our fatigue with every sloshing step.

Despite my initial reticence to return to Thon Buri, the unrelenting miseries of the jungle wilds made the city's outskirts a welcome sight as my heart filled with joy in anticipation of a night's sleep with a roof over my head at long last! Yet I tempered my exuberance and approached Thon Buri with the greatest timidity, using only the roughshod paths that had been carved by local rice farmers and staying well clear of the main arteries of commerce which I fully expected to be closely watched by the soldiers of the new regime. This roundabout navigation proved to be a wise choice for one mile from the city I detected something unnerving through my watch glass: the flag of General Thong Duang's army raised high above the Royal palace, fluttering in the rain-saturated wind. I slowly closed my watch glass, my hands shaking as I compressed its rungs shut whilst simultaneously turning about and calling for Tuk.

"How may I be of service, Sir." Tuk responded, the look on his face informing me that he had detected the look of anxiety that was plastered about mine.

"I need to beg you a difficult favor, my friend. Disguise yourself as a merchantman or as a peasant and reconnoiter Thon Buri. The flag of Thong Duang is flying above the palace and I fear that something afoul is at foot. The

men and I will retrace our steps back to the
hamlet that we steered clear of five miles ago.
We will take it by force and use it as a refuge
while awaiting your return. I will look forward
to your report most eagerly, Tuk. Be cautious
but do not delay. We cannot remain undetected
in this land for long and our lives may all be
in danger."

"I won't disappoint you, Sir." Tuk stated as he
stood at attention and saluted me.

　　The peasants of Jo Jo village had never
seen white men before and they stood petrified
as my heavily armed mercenaries entered their
muddy home brandishing our weapons, herding the
villagers into the tiny Buddhist wat that
occupied the hamlet's center and holding them
captive to prevent potential spies from
divulging our location to the authorities. I
ordered First Sergeant Loril to establish a
defensive perimeter about the village's
periphery. Under First Sergeant's drunken, but
nonetheless able, direction my eighty-four
mercenaries, all seasoned combat veterans by
now—forty men of the original company having
succumbed to battle wounds and disease—moved
into their tactical positions like pawns being
controlled by a chess master, silently waiting
in their concealments, ready to strike at a
moment's notice. The men and I waited for two
days, two miserable and anxious days, our minds
spinning and our bodies begging for action to
alleviate the mental anguish of the unknown. On
the night of the second day, a rather comically
dressed Tuk rode into the village dressed in
dirty peasant's rags, riding on an oxcart that
was drawn by two large, filthy, heavily bearded
oxen, the cart filled with large pots of rice
and barrels of liquor.

"Any fares for the fine gentlemen?" Tuk asked
with a broad smile, choking on his own laughter
as he spoke.

"I was beginning to think that you'd been killed, my good man. What news do you bring from Thon Buri?" I inquired as my foul mood lifted.

"Only bad news, I'm afraid. King Taaksin fell into a fit of melancholy again, three fortnights ago, and the nobles used the king's illness as an opportunity to conspire against him in conjunction with the commander of the Thon Buri garrison, General Phyra San. Phyra San declared himself king, but when news of the coup reached General Thong Duang, Thong Duang marched his army on Thon Buri and defeated Phyra San, who has been executed at the hands of Thong Duang himself. The nobles all fled the city, fearing that Thong Duang would return Taaksin to power and that they would be punished for their treachery. General Thong Duang caught the nobles as they attempted to flee aboard junks, but instead of exacting revenge, Thong Duang made a pact with them to make himself king. Newly anointed, King Thong Duang led the procession of nobles to the prison where Taaksin was held. He ordered the guards to open Taaksin's cell and King Taaksin rose from the ground with his arms held open to embrace his old friend. The nobles were all sweating, sweating as traitors do when confronted with their crimes, fearing that Thong Duang had tricked them into a murderous trap. Thong Duang entered the prison cell, his arms spread open to embrace Taaksin but…"

"What man, speak!" I demanded as I watched a trickle of tears starting to wind its way down Tuk's face.

"…Thong Duang unsheathed his krabi and sliced Taaksin's head off!" Tuk shrieked hysterically as his body swayed, nearly falling off his oxcart and onto the ground as I steadied him with all the might that my arms could muster.

"My country is ruined! We have given so much blood to rebuild the kingdom, so much blood for nothing! Now Thai are killing Thai and everything we have fought for is lost!"

"Come now, I grieve for Taaksin as much as you do, he was a dear friend and a close ally. But all was not for naught, General Thong Duang is a harsh man but he is a loyal Thai and he will never allow your kingdom to bow to the forces of another nation, especially not the Burmese, who he despises at least as much as Taaksin did. That I do not care for Thong Duang is well-known, but even I must admit that he is an able commander. Though I loved Taaksin, his eccentricities were extreme and perhaps a more modest and level-headed monarch will do well by your country in the end."

"But he murdered my king!" Tuk wept uncontrollably as he spoke.

"That is the way of kings, my valiant friend. To rule is to murder, whether by war or by intrigue. I am sure that a man of your talents will prove invaluable to your country no matter what regime sits in the palace. Thong Duang is a tyrant, but a pragmatic tyrant, and he will welcome the loyal servants of Siam back into his fold once this dark storm blows over. I'm sure that you and your family will be quite safe, quite safe and quite prosperous."

"No, I live to serve King Taaksin and no other! There is no Siam for me now, you must take me with you! I have brought food and drink for your men, I killed a man and stole his cart to bring it to you! You must not abandon me, please, I beg you!"

"I will not abandon you Tuk, we will speak on this matter with clearer heads in the morrow. For now, sleep, my loyal friend."

CHAPTER 15
Escape from Siam

The unnatural tranquility engulfing the captive village was interrupted only by the eager gum smacking of my famished mercenaries as they devoured the rations that had been procured by Tuk, eating their meals whilst stationed at their guard posts, their weapons held close and at the ready. With the men distracted, I gathered my cadre to inform them of Tuk's discovery—that Siam's government was now firmly in the grasp of General Thong Duang. I was relieved to find the cadre to be of the unanimous estimation that our contract had been with King Taaksin and that his death had freed us from the remainder of our service obligation. This judgment left us with only one question, one rather difficult question: how to escape from The Kingdom of Siam with our lives.

"If we march east, retracing our steps through Cambodia and from there marching onward to Conchin-China, we can petition the French in Hanoi City for passage to Europe." I suggested, reluctantly, as I wracked my aching mind for a solution to our dangerous dilemma, desperately straining to concoct a reasonable escape plan. I knew full well that the odds were heavily stacked against us. "Thong Duang will not take the breaking of our contract lightly; he will certainly pursue us, out of pride if not for vengeance. Thong Duang has resented our presence since we first stepped foot in Siam and he will gladly accept any excuse to execute us."

"But de Conchinese iz hostile to Siam, what will stop dem from attacking us at de border where we cross?" First Sergeant Loril observed. He was unusually sober tonight.

"Yes and traveling north is similarly uninviting. We'd starve before we made it over the mountains into China. To the West lie the Burmese who will gladly shoot any man who dares to cross their heavily fortified border." I stated pessimistically.

"Then south to Malay Land where the Dutch hold sway. We have more than enough gold to buy passage to Europe several times over." Suggested Dr. Watkins, a man whom all present held in the highest esteem for his intelligence and cool-headedness.

"My dear doctor, Tuk has just informed us that the southern provinces are in the midst of revolution and that Thong Duang is preparing, preparing at this very moment, to attack their usurper prince. If we march south we will risk being trapped between two hostile armies whereas in the east we need only fear one." I replied, not keen on the idea of leading my men straight into the tiger's mouth.

"Sir, if I may, the trip south is shorter by several hundred miles and the men are already suffering from foot and groin rot, courtesy of this unrelenting rain. The doctor is of the opinion that a plague of malaria is not far off for the disease is blown in from the sea by the monsoon winds every single year and no one is spared from its wrath." Lieutenant Macellaro offered meekly, yet with conviction in his eyes as Doctor Watkins nodded gently in agreement.

"I know the south, Sir. My family is from a village near Phuket, which is not a far march. British and Dutch ships call on the port regularly, mostly the British since the start of the Anglo-Dutch War, but many of the ships belong to traders who's only political allegiance is to gold." Tuk suggested loudly in his always impeccable and accent-free English. It was the first time that I had ever heard my

trusted interpreter state an opinion with such
force and my cadre and I listened to him with
the greatest of attentions.

"Can you show us safe passage to this Phuket,
Tuk?" I asked hopefully, the prospect of
shortening our journey through the miserable
jungles lightening my heavy heart.

"Safe, no. But it is safer than our other
alternatives."

"Whatever course we take, it will be one that
is decided upon unanimously. If any man objects
to the southern route, let him speak now." I
demanded.

There was not a word of dissent from any
of my cadre, only nervous anticipation of the
challenges of the perilous journey on which we
were about to embark. I dismissed my cadre with
stern orders to generously nourish their bodies
with both food and drink and to have the men
formed-up and ready to commence marching at
sunset. As the sun dipped below the Siamese
horizon, we tied the doors and windows of the
village temple tightly shut, the captive
villagers sitting huddled in the temple's
corner shaking with fear, our hemp ties buying
time for our escape as my mercenary company and
I slipped down the jungle trails as quietly as
shadows disappearing into the night, Tuk
leading our way.

Sleeping in the snake, mosquito, and
leech-infested jungle whilst the battering sun
roasted the waterlogged earth, we traveled only
at night, stepping carefully to avoid the
deadly cobras which traversed the jungle floors
with monarchial impunity. The third night of
our hellish march, one of my mercenaries was
ambushed by a devilish, striped tiger which
mauled the helpless man's body beyond
recognition before the beast was felled by the

blast of a dozen muskets, fired simultaneously and shredding the evil creature into a half dozen pieces. The audacity of the tiger's attack compelled me to require that any man pausing to use the bushes be accompanied by two of his armed comrades for protection. To add insult to injury, the moisture-saturated jungle was rotting the flesh off of our tortured feet and many of my men began marching barefoot, unable to tolerate the friction of their boots, a situation that only exacerbated the danger from the jungle's many poisonous snakes and biting parasites, multiplying our already nearly intolerable burden of disabled men who were in need of assistance while marching. As if these challenges were not enough, the pestilence of malaria struck just as Doctor Watkins had foretold, a pestilence of sickly airs that was tracked in by the monsoon winds. We were forced to lose a full night of travel to fashion bamboo stretchers to carry those of us too weakened by the evil humors to ambulate. As such, the news from Tuk, news delivered in the middle of our second week of travel, that we were now only one night's march from Phuket provided a much needed boost to our sagging morale. As the sun began to peak above the horizon, I moved our formation off of the narrow bush trails and into the hidden depths of the dark jungle—then I called my cadre to conference.

"Tuk's village is less than a day's march ahead, only five hours march if we were to take the main roads. The village is located on the shore below that steep precipice, that rocky crag in the distance that was only just visible in the daylight. Tuk is of the opinion that it would be prudent to approach his village with caution for the local strongman is allied with the usurper prince who now rules this territory and he may look upon us as enemies if we are discovered. I propose that we scale the precipice and reconnoiter the village by

looking glass to make certain that it is free
of hostiles before revealing ourselves. We can
then enter the village and use Tuk's family
connections to barter for transportation to the
British trading post on the Isle of Phuket,
which Tuk says is readily accessible by a short
boat ride. Phuket is controlled by the British
Army so there is little to fear from the
Siamese once we make landfall there. Our only
danger in Phuket will be of the European
variety. In Phuket, we must play strongly on
the fact that we are employed by a British
company, a company that is chartered in the
British-allied Kingdom of Portugal. I do not
think that the British will give us trouble but
we must guard ourselves closely against
diarrhea of the tongue for many of our
mercenaries have fought against King George in
the past—myself included—and I must impress
upon you all that it would be highly imprudent
to reveal this! Counsel your men in the
harshest terms, there is no room for error.
That is all." I concluded my orders and
dismissed my cadre back to their soldiers as we
prepared to embark on what we prayed would be
the final leg of our long journey.

     The men chopped our path through the
thick jungle vines and the waist-high, razor-
sharp elephant grasses for there were no trails
leading to our destination: the steep,
solitary, narrow mount that overlooked Tuk's
village. We advanced as silently as possible,
not a word uttered by a single man,
communicating only by hand signals. Our strict
adherence to noise discipline proved its value
when we suddenly heard the boom of cannon and
the report of musket fire in the near distance.
The men redoubled their efforts, hacking at the
grass with the gusto of gardening fanatics.

     The precipice was a towering heap of
great boulders that rose abruptly from the
surrounded sea of jungle at a seventy degree

angle on four of its five sides, the fifth side
a more modest, yet still daunting, slope of
fifty-five degree. I ordered my men to set up a
defensive perimeter at the base of the mount
whilst the cadre and I scaled its least
imposing face, a climb which proved exceedingly
perilous. We looked on in helpless horror as
Lieutenant Ara Macellaro lost his footing on a
patch of loose rocks and plummeted two hundred
feet, his life ripped away from him in an
instant, his lifeless cadaver lying contorted
on the boulders below. Helio Macellaro and
Doctor Watkins immediately climbed down in a
panicked frenzy, but there was nothing that
could be done: nothing, save for pray.

A lone, twisted rattan grew perched atop
the mighty rock heap and my exhausted cadre and
I indulged in this singular tree's merciful
shade, the drooping leaves of which provided
some degree of shelter from the peltering
monsoon showers that had started, yet again,
after an ever-so-brief respite, a pause just
long enough to allow the sun's radiance to
broil the air into an intolerable mix of raw
heat and suffocating humidity. Through my oft-
fogging looking glass, First Sergeant Loril,
Tuk, and I bore sight of a great battle taking
place less than a mile to the east of Tuk's
village. The village's bamboo huts appeared
intact and without evident damage, much to
Tuk's relief for he still had several blood-
relations residing there.

The battle between the two Siamese
armies, one commanded by King Thong Duang and
bearing modern European firearms, the other
under the control of the rebellious southern
prince and armed only with traditional Siamese
weaponry, was one of the most horrific contests
I ever witnessed, fought with such wonton
brutality that it rivaled the frontier wars in
the American Colonies. The armies clashed for
hours, men falling like corn before the

reaper's blade until the usurper prince was
forced to accept that his army was no match for
the modern cannon and muskets of Thong Duang.
The rebel prince led a final suicidal charge
directed straight at the center of Thong
Duang's formation. Row-after-row of the
prince's men were cut down by grape shot and
canister fire that roared out of the smoking
barrels of Thong Duang's cannon, blasting
gaping holes in the southern army's lines and
littering the battlefield with casualties. Yet
surprisingly, the prince's tenacious army
continued their advance through this maelstrom
of lead, seemingly oblivious to the slaughter
that was occurring about them, reaching the
Royal Siamese Army's lines and crashing into
them, tearing a wide breech into the middle of
Thong Duang's formation. The screams of the
royal soldiers intermixed with the dying
rumbles of their muskets as the imperial
soldiers were decapitated by the krabi-wielding
rebels and impaled at the end of the southern
army's spears. In a strategic redeployment,
Thong Duang collapsed his flanks to plug the
break in his formation as the usurper prince
simultaneously ordered his men to withdraw. The
sun beginning to set, the two bloodied and
exhausted foes withdrew from the field of
battle.

Using the darkness of the night as cover,
my men and I crept out of the bush and snuck
through the battlefield, crawling over the
bodies of the dead and the dying. As the sun
began its ascent, we hurried towards the sea,
encountering three heavily armed scouts from
Thong Duang's army less than a mile from the
shore and slaughtering them with musket fire
before the scouts had realized that we were
upon them. I shuddered at the sound of our
weapons, knowing that the commotion would draw
the rest of Thong Duang's scouting party in our
direction, praying that we would find
fishermen's crafts to commandeer before Thong

Duang realized that my mercenaries and I were located in such precariously close proximity. Cutting our way through the now thinning jungle scrub, we reached the calm turquoise waters of the Indian Ocean and, thank be to the heavens, a dozen longboats scattered about, their owners hiding with their families from the warring carnage that had engulfed their home.

I needn't give the order. My men immediately scrambled to task, turning over six of the longboats and pushing them out to sea. The fishing boats were large and sturdy, built from tough jungle wood. We began rowing as mice scurry from a hungry cat, rowing in the direction that Tuk directed us as he shouted his navigation loudly across the rocking sea. Halfway to the Isle of Phuket—a sweltering, tropical bastion of European dominion—my men and I spotted three longboats full of Siamese soldiers pursuing us in the distance. My men rowed with even greater tenacity, increasing our lead as we ran scared from the tightly packed enemy boats that were energetically chasing our wake. Finally, land. We pulled ashore onto the white sand beaches of the Isle of Phuket and abandoned our longboats as we fled into the jungle thicks, dense bush where we laid quietly in ambush, nervously awaiting our pursuers. Thong Duang's scouting party arrived, a group of terrifying Royal Tigers, hardened combat veterans, each Royal Tiger armed with a musket, two pistols, and twin krabi. I whispered for my mercenaries to hold their fire while the Siamese grounded their boats. As the enemy began their brazen, swaggering advance towards the jungle, I shouted for my men to unloose their muskets, a ferocious volley of hot lead erupting from the tree line that left not a single one of Thong Duang's scouts standing. Silence filled the air as the powder smoke wafted clear into the sea breeze, a silence interrupted only by the death cries of the Royal Tigers who now lay dying on the beach as the new day's sun beat down upon them from over the rattan-studded horizon, the last morning of their short lives.

My mercenaries and I emerged from the jungle, free men at last. We found our way into Phuket Town to barter for passage to Europe. I slept for two days, such was my exhaustion, my men following suit, sleeping on the white sand beaches outside of town by choice, a soldiers' preference, sleeping under the starlight and next to the gently rolling sea. Finally recovered after my long sleep and several hardy meals, I began to compile an account of my journeys under the shade of the beach palms. After years of bloody toiling, I now found myself with nothing but free time on my hands as my men and I waited impatiently for a passing merchantman or whaler, a wait that we knew might extend for weeks or even months. I opened my journal, a blank book which I had purchased in Quebec City but which I had never found the peace of mind to begin. I put my pen to the white paper and began to tell my rollicking tale while praying that my life of adventure had drawn to an end.

CHAPTER 16
Life After Siam

Though the cost of our passage aboard the English whaler, *The Drunken Whore*, was extortionist, the officers I had crammed our satchels so full with plunder from our Siamese campaigns that we still arrived in Portugal as wealthy men, wealthy men made even richer by the three years of pay that was owed to us by Mr. Jacobs. After a week of celebration in the pubs and brothels of Lisbon, my cadre and I parted ways whilst swearing unending oaths of loyalty to one another and heartfelt promises to keep in contact wherever life might find us. First Sergeant Loril continued his life as a mercenary, though he could have easily afforded to retire. My hard fighting, hard drinking First Sergeant so craved the excitement of combat that the man found civilian life intolerably mundane, wholly unfulfilling. First Sergeant Loril found his way to India where he wrote me letters every few months, letters to which I always eagerly replied, letters that told of several heroic engagements in which my good friend managed to entangle himself until finally meeting his end in the sky-scraping mountains of the hinterlands that are known as Afghan Land. This rugged crossroads of history, located along the ancient silk road, has long attracted warriors of the highest caliber—Alexander the Great and Genghis Khan to name a few—and I firmly believe that First Sergeant Loril would have been proud to know that he would end his life's journey amongst such renowned company.

Doctor Lance Watkins vowed to never practice medicine again, the kindly man driven from his once beloved profession by long years of treating combat casualties, jungle rot, cholera, and louse infestations, conditions which plague all field armies but which bred in especially horrible incarnations in the hot and wet jungles of Indochina. The doctor's decision to put down his medicine bag was cemented when Mr. Jacobs, our boisterous employer, quietly asked the sea-weary physician (immediately after our return from Siam, before we had even had a night of rest or a meal) for a second opinion on a medical condition that had weakened his body to such a degree that I now hardly recognized my employer, his once plethoric face now taut and emaciated, his portly belly vanished as if into thin air. Though exhausted from our voyage and not yet unpacked, Doctor Watkins dutifully inspected his employer, confirming the diagnosis of the Plague of Venus, syphilis. Worse yet, upon physical inspection of the man's genitals, my loyal doctor-friend had the unfortunate duty of informing Mr. Jacobs that he had contracted not one disease of the passion, but two, the doctor finding our employer's penis infested with the thick puss of gonorrhea, an evil humor referred to in the vernacular as 'the clap' for those afflicted must clap their hands about their penis to dislodge caked pus before they can expel their water.

Now in no condition to manage his enterprises, Mr. Jacobs offered me the prospect of purchasing his mercenary business, an offer which, after conferring with Helio Macellaro and Doctor Watkins, I accepted with my brave Lieutenant and the upstanding doctor as co-investors. I settled in Portugal and renewed contact with my family via post, the civilian sea lanes having returned to normalcy after the signing of the Treaty of Paris between Britain and the newly recognized United States of America. My brother, Light Horse Harry (as Henry was now known), responded to my letters some months later with the regrettable news that my beloved parents had made the journey into the divine, a revelation that I took

harshly, nearly reverting to the escape of
drunkenness and only saved from that dreadful
abyss by the unwavering support of my business
partners. On a happier note, Henry informed me
that my old arch-nemeses, First Sergeant Miller
and his Indian lackey, Wolfslayer, had been
convicted and subsequently hung on charges of
sedition after attempting to sell American
battle plans to the British some months after I
had fled from the Colonies into Canada. My
treacherous old commander, Colonel Woodrow, had
met a similarly untimely end: shot dead during
a gentlemen's duel by his executive officer, a
duel fought over the Colonel's brutal
methodology and his second-in-command's refusal
to endorse it.

Through the years, my brother had rapidly
scaled the ranks of government in Virginia,
first serving in The General Assembly of
Virginia and later proudly attaining the office
of governor, a fact which lifted my heart for I
remained a proud Virginian and a proud Lee. In
1794, at the twilight of his term as governor,
Henry co-commanded, alongside elderly General
Washington, a 13,000 strong militia that had
been hastily recruited by The Federal
Government in response to the anti-federalist
Whiskey Rebellion[25], a heathen uprising of the
lowest classes in the far-reaches of Appalachia
against a tax levied on distilled spirits.
Though the ailing General Washington served as
the militia's figurehead, it was widely known
that Henry was the man who was truly
responsible for crushing the uprising, a

25. Whiskey Rebellion: A revolt against a tax on whiskey
    that was centered in Western Pennsylvania but which
    extended, to varying degrees, throughout all of
    Appalachia where whiskey was a prime source of extra
    income for farmers. The Whiskey Rebellion was
    crushed by General George Washington's and General
    Henry Lee's militia, thus establishing the primacy
    of Federal control over the states, boosting the
    confidence of the citizens of The United States of
    America in their new Federal Government.

victory that had preserved his nascent country and saved it from fracturing and descending into anarchy.

In 1799, a grateful electorate of eastern landowners propelled Henry into the United States House of Representatives, the lower chamber of the newly adopted bicameral legislature, a legislature designed in the Constitution of 1787[26] to preserve the power of the larger and more populous states whilst protecting the sovereignty of their smaller brethren. As a United States Congressman, my dear brother was able to use his influence to clear my name and to obtain a full and unconditional pardon from President Thomas Jefferson, a family acquaintance and the brilliant author of The Declaration of Independence, a document that the great man had authored while he was still in his youthful twenties.

26. Constitution of 1787: Drafted to rectify the deficiencies of the original constitution—The Articles of Confederation—The Constitution of the United States of America was ratified on June 21, 1788. Under the new constitution, the government of The United States is divided into three branches: the executive branch, the judicial branch, and the legislative branch. The legislative branch is further subdivided into a The Senate and The House of Representatives, the consequence of a compromise between the larger and the smaller states that is known as 'The Connecticut Compromise,' a political settlement whereby each state, regardless of population, is entitled to two representatives to the upper chambers of the legislature (known as 'senators') and in which the number of representatives to the lower chambers (known as 'congressmen') are apportioned according to the size of a state's population.

My own life during this period was gloriously mundane, a much needed respite after the swash-buckling excitement of my youth. I married a Portuguese girl, the beautiful niece of my business partner, Helio Macellaro, but alas she passed away during the birth of our first child, the poor babe accompanying his mother to the grave. I grieved the loss of my loved ones by dedicating myself wholly to my enterprises—a dedication to work that transformed me into a wealthy and, more importantly, busy man who was far too preoccupied to have time to waste on self-pity. Nonetheless, as the years flew by, I found myself molested by a craving to return to the free-spirited ways of my youth, a thirst for military adventure that incessantly tickled my mind, a perseveration that grew stronger by the day. As such, it was with great enthusiasm that I received the following letter from Henry one calm Portuguese morning:

September 29, 1800

Dearest brother,

I write to you not as family, but rather in my capacity as a Representative of the Great State of Virginia to The United States Congress. Our nation, in its financially troubled state of weakness, has tired of the illegal and unprovoked extortion of the infidel corsairs of the Barbary States. The Barbary Sultanates, the vilest of which is the Sultanate of Tripoli, led by the blood-thirsty pirate, Pasha Karamanli, have emptied our coffers with their incessant demands for protection monies, monies demanded at the threat of the destruction our peaceful merchantmen and the impressment of our sailors into lives of slavery under the infidel's yolk. Just last year—and much to my disdain—our old family friend, President Jefferson, agreed to pay Pasha Karamanli $18,000/year as tribute to guarantee the safe passage of our seamen in the waters of the Mediterranean. Yet even this amount has failed to appease the wicked corsair and Karamanli now demands an additional $225,000 ransom, a fee which our nation could not afford even if our pride would permit it (our entire tax base is only $10 million!).

To counter this vile threat, President Jefferson has ordered the construction of six frigates, a fleet which is now preparing to embark on a mission to cripple the Tripolitan corsairs and to return the rule of law to the Mediterranean Sea. To aid this mission, our nation requires mercenary forces to bolster our small detachment of marines which will accompany the above said fleet. The President and I have recommended your fine company to Congress and it is our hope that you will agree to provide soldiers of quality to serve The United States of America in this capacity. Congress has agreed to compensate you with a stipend of $11,000/year should your company find the proposed undertaking worthwhile.

I hope this letter finds you well, please respond immediately.

Sincerely,
Henry

As my eyes scanned the page with unbridled excitement, I shouted for Helio Macellaro and Doctor Watkins, both of whom came sprinting into the room, Helio holding kitchen knife and Doctor Watkins a chair, raised above his head as if he were about to strike.

"Why all the commotion, Jonathan? We feared that we were being burglarized only to find you looking as giddy as a child on Christmas morning!" Said the doctor as he put down the chair and pushed his spectacles up his narrow nose.

"No, Lance, I'm as eager as a soldier preparing for battle! My brother has arranged for a contract with The United States for an $11,000 per year stipend in return for our services in a brewing war against the Barbary Pirates."

"Eleven thousand American dollars, humph; given the wretched state of the American economy I can't help but wonder if those dollars will be worthless by the time we actually receive them. I know he is your brother, Jonathan, but we mustn't let family sentiments undermine our business sense. We only have one company of the regiment available at the present and the offer from the Malay Prince would be paid in gold, gold that will not devalue like American paper."

"Yes, but you and I are getting too old to be traveling half-way across the globe and I know that you're itching for a fight as badly as I. If we entertain this American proposition, we can lead our mercenaries, you and I. Think of it, one last fight for two old soldiers, a fight that is sitting right on our doorstep, just across the Straits of Gibraltar!"

"And leave Helio to manage our enterprises on his own?"

"I am more than able," replied my fiery Portuguese business partner. "Go off and have your adventure, old men! I'll convert the American dollars into sterling as soon I

receive them to protect us against their fickle
politics. I run this business most of the time
anyway, I just pretend like you're the ones who
make the decisions!"

My good-natured business partners and I
broke away early that evening to further
discuss Henry's proposition over a hearty meal
and glasses of stout port wine. Though we all
conceded that sending our available troops to
Malay Land would be more profitable than
contracting with the Americans, Doctor Watkins
and I could not conceal our eagerness for one
last adventure and Helio, supportive as ever,
did not object. The issue now decided, Doctor
Watkins and I would put to sea for one last
fight, a fight that we would undertake in the
service of the country that had sent me into
exile fleeing the hangman's noose so many years
before. My business partners and I sat down
that night to write Henry our affirmative
reply. The ink had barely begun to drying on
our postal before we were galloping down the
roads of Lisbon to our mercenary army's
training grounds, giddy to begin the
preparations for the brewing crusade against
the corsairs of the Maghreb

CHAPTER 17
War in the Mediterranean

February 1804: Years of idle waiting tore mercilessly at my shriveled soul, so did I yearn to taste that evil elixir of youth, unbridled combat. The American navy bombs Tripoli then batters a smattering of enemy corsairs ships before retiring to the posh comfort of the Port of Lisbon, a safe-haven provided for America's fleet by none other than myself for I was instrumental in convincing Principe Joao—the regent ruler of Portugal—to order the Portuguese fleet to secure the Straits of Gibraltar against pirate incursions into the Atlantic. The American's drop their anchor and wait for orders from home, orders that are never received before the Tripolitans have repaired their damaged fleets and patched the walls of their massive harbor fortress in preparation for the next seaborne assault. The war had become a vicious cycle of senseless actions, minor engagements which bring America no closer to victory and which see my highly trained mercenaries wasting away in boredom in their training camp, preparing day-after-day for a fight which they now doubt will ever come.

In mid-February news arrived, dreary news, but not unwelcome news for any perturbation in the dullness of the Barbary War was by that time viewed as a blessed change of pace from the nail biting monotony of the training camp. I had read the news in a Portuguese newspaper—being quite fluent in the tongue of my adopted country by then—read with disbelief as I learnt that the *U.S.S. Philadelphia*, a powerful forty-four gun American frigate, had run aground against a shoal in Tripoli harbor and had been captured by the Tripolitans. The story continued as remarkably as it had begun, expounding on the heroism of Lieutenant Stephen Decatur, who had led a party of marines aboard the captive *U.S.S. Philadelphia* and lit her afire, depriving the Tripolitan's of their stolen treasure, depriving the enemy of a powerful weapon of war. I smiled in frustration as I cursed my lot in life, stuck on shore so far from the action that the battles in the Mediterranean might as well have been occurring in the bleakest corner of Siberia. I exited my comfortable office and then trotted down the shiny brass railed staircase that led outside onto Lisbon's sunny streets. I climbed into my coach and ordered my servant—one of my servants for I had many—to make for the training fields, my heart downtrodden at the prospect of another day of pointless battle drills.

September 1804: The unexpected arrival of Captain William Eaton, his executive officer Lieutenant Presley O'Bannon, and a platoon of rugged-appearing American marines stirred my glacially tranquil military camp into an uproar of excitement. The American entourage stalked across the parade grounds and barged into my command tent with such force that I dropped my salad fork onto the floor as I slung out the twin pistols that I perpetually kept holstered to my sides, even whilst strolling about Lisbon's finer quarters, a brazen violation of Portuguese law that my wealth and influence permitted me. Seeing that the intruders were Americans—Americans dressed in the navy blue, gold-trimmed, sea-smelling uniforms of the marines—I lowered my weapons and began to chastise the men for their rude entrance.

"What in damnation gives you the right to trample into my command post, unannounced! Were you raised in a henhouse or bred by wild savages!" I spouted as an awakened dragon spews fire from his mouth. "Forgive me, Captain, but you nearly just caught two lead balls into your fancy uniform!"

"My apologies, it's been a hectic day," Captain Eaton responded as he sat down in a chair that I had not yet offered to him. "We just got word that a good friend of mine has died and a whole lot of other marines alongside him. Yeah, just yesterday, good ole Richard…Captain Richard Somers…and his executive officer, Lieutenant Henry Wadsworth. They set out on some damn fool mission to try and plant a ketch full of powder beneath Tripoli's harbor fortress, planning to drop anchor and then blow the ketch from a distance. Didn't work out that way though; the Dirty Camel's spotted them and blew their boat sky high right outta the water. Thirteen fine marines dead, just like that." Captain Eaton informed me as he struck a match on his impeccably shined boots and then lit a comically long Cuban cigar that hung out of his mustached mouth like a branch off of a willow tree. I didn't come here to cry about dead friends though, Mr. Lee; I came here to inform you that your expensive mercenaries finally have a mission."

"You have my full and undivided attention, Captain, do go on," I said, the excitement evident in my voice.

"By the authority of the President of the United States of America, I order your mercenaries to accompany me to Alexandria, Egypt. In Egypt we will join forces with the militia of Hamet Karamanli and then we will march our army across the desert to put an end to this little war."

"I thought that Karamanli already ruled Tripoli, am I missing something?"

"Wrong Karamanli, you're thinking of Yusuf Karamanli. The fellow I'm talking about is his older brother and he's not happy about the way his little brother, that's Yusuf, deposed him off the throne and then exiled him away to Egypt twenty years ago. The diplomats have done us a favor, for once, and gotten this former Dirty Camel king so deep into our pants' pocket that he's fingering our balls. All we have to do to end this war is to march straight into Tripoli and place his sandy ass back on the throne, just like that."

I stood from my seat and vigorously shook Captain Eaton's firm hand, a smile of joy pasted across my face as I called my mercenaries into formation and announced our mission. My troops erupted into great cries of exuberance as they set off at a frantic pace to begin packing their rucksacks for the expedition. Before the next dawn's sun had broken over the Portuguese hills, my men and I were tossing about the Mediterranean aboard three American frigates: *U.S.S. Argus*, *U.S.S. Hornet*, and *U.S.S. Natilus*.

April 1804: Trekking hundreds-upon-hundreds of miles through the bone rotting Sahara failed to even begin to demoralize our hodgepodge army, so eager were the men and the officers for the fight that lay ahead. At the head of our column, Captain Eaton rode with Pasha Hamet Karamanli—a slovenly man who was dressed in Arab's robes, robes that stunk to high heavens with the eldest Karamanli's putrid body odor, so potent was his smell that I sincerely believe that Pasha Hamet had never taken a bath in his entire life. Behind our leaders marched Captain Eaton's ten marines followed by Pasha Hamet's hundred Arab militiamen, hard-faced Bedouins who had lived lives filled with tribal warfare, no strangers to the crack of the musket or to the work of the saber. My mercenaries and I, two hundred strong in all—one hundred men paid for by the United States Government plus an additional one hundred men whom I had volunteered free of charge—marched in the rear of the battle column, a position which suited me for it allowed me to keep my eyes on the Arab militia, men whom both Captain Eaton and I were loath to trust. Three hundred in total, our small army raced off in pursuit of Yusuf Karamanli's eastern commander, Hassan Bey, and his army of four thousand corsairs. As we marched over what must have been the thousandth sand dune, Captain Eaton and Hamet Karamanli suddenly halted and ordered their men to lie behind the dunes as they quickly turning their camels about and sprinted toward me.

"What's the matter, Captain?" I inquired as I ordered my men to take a knee in the hot sand.

"We spotted the town of Derna in the distance, can't be more than two miles to the North."

"Is our fleet visible on the horizon?"

Before Captain Eaton could speak, my question was answered by the booming of sea cannon followed by the exploding of shells over the fortress-town of Derna.

"How long do you plan to let the fleet soften their defenses?" I probed, hoping that the brazen Marine would allow ample time for our fleet to weaken the target; despite the excellent quality of our army we were greatly outnumbered.

"The Admiral plans on twelve hours of suppression fire and then we commence the assault. I'm sending the Pasha's men to take the residential sector and the marketplace; your mercenaries and my marines will attack the fortress."

"Understood, my men and I eagerly await your command!"

At precisely the tick of the twelfth
hour, with the sun sitting low in the sky,
Captain Eaton waved his mameluk[27] forward as he
charged over the sand dunes, followed closely
behind by his loyal Leathernecks[28]. I ordered my
mercenaries to follow the marines' lead,
finding my command met by a roaring war cry as
my battle-hungry soldiers fixed their bayonets
and charged over the baking dunes. The corsair
artillery in their fortress had long since been
silenced by the mighty guns of our fleet and
the fortress' walls had fared no better,
collapsing in several locations into great gaps
that my men poured through like ants invading a
rival colony.

Inside the dying fortress, I beheld a
dreadfully wonderful sight: hundreds of
corsairs gasping their last breaths, their
bodies mangled by the shrapnel from our sea
cannon, many of them lying crushed under the
weight of the fortress' fallen walls, walls
that they had huddled behind for protection but
which had instead sealed their mortal fates. My
men and I rushed forward into the fortress,
shooting and slashing our way through a sea of
frightened moor-skinned corsairs, corsairs
dressed in dark green bandanas, white short
pants, and gold-laced red vests without
undershirts, armed with jagged knives and
Ottoman pistols with heavy brass butts. But the

27. Mameluk: A curved Arabian sword, similar to a
    scimitar. Favored by pirates and marines because it
    is easy to wield in tight spaces, such as in a
    ship's hold.

28. Leathernecks: The marines were referred to by the
    American sailors as 'leathernecks' for their habit
    of wearing high collars made of thick cattle hide to
    protect their necks whilst storming enemy vessels.
    The thick leather provided excellent protection
    against flying shrapnel, a frequent hazard of naval
    combat, and provided some protection against saber
    swipes, especially from enemies cutting down at them
    from the riggings overhead.

corsair's weapons failed them as their fortress had. By the break of dawn, Tripolitan bodies crowded the grounds of Derna, at least two thousand corsairs lying dead, a stark contrast to our army's mere dozen casualties which included: two marines—dead; three mercenaries—two dead, one dying; and seven of Pasha Hamet's Arab militiamen—five dead, two afflicted with saber wounds to the abdomen and legs.

Though our soldiers begged for a respite, Captain Eaton and I whipped them back to work at preparing defensive fortifications, both of us knowing well that Yusuf Karamanli's general, Hassan Bey, still roamed the deserts with an army of over a thousand corsairs. The Tripolitan counterattack came at noon. The sun beat down upon the battlefield as the corsairs, with the aid of their field artillery, pushed us back from Derna town and into the fortress. But the corsair's success would be their undoing for they were now in range of our fleet's cannon. The pirates found themselves trapped in a pit of death as metal hell raining down upon them from our ships cannon, cannon fire that was complemented by my men's staccato sniping from our fortress perch. As the sun began to set, Captain Eaton and I led a spirited bayonet charge into Derna town and Hassan Bey's forces disintegrated before us, fleeing into the desert wastelands.

June 1805: Treachery! The *U.S.S. Constellation* arrived with the most loathsome news: The United States of America has signed a peace treaty with Yusuf Karamanli! I stood bewildered as I read the terms of peace, squinting to read the document through the vicious sandstorm that had suddenly engulfed Derna, sand blowing so hard that it seeped around the edges of the closed windows, clouding the air and coating my command post with a fine layer of choking white dust. Unbelievably, The United States had agreed to exchange three hundred American prisoners-of-war for one hundred captive pirates plus a bounty of sixty thousand dollars, sixty thousand dollars that would be added to the endless list of extortions that four years of war had been fought to terminate! I glanced at Captain Eaton, the hardened marine, and saw him trembling hot with rage.

"Damn those politicians! We fought a revolution to get rid of the British aristocrats and now we've bred our own! Damn easy to sign a peace treaty when you're sitting comfortably behind your desk sipping your morning tea with nothing to worry about but the next election!" Captain Eaton snarled, spitting out a juicy wad of tobacco from the inside of his cheek onto the sand-grimed floor.

"Did any orders for the army arrive along with this farcical peace treaty?" I begged.

"Aye, we're ordered to pack up and make for the ships within the next three days. The men will be heartbroken…"

"It's not the men that I'm worried about. When Pasha Hamet gets news of our betrayal he'll turn his guns against us. His forces have swollen to nearly one thousand Bedouins, rugged men who look like they know how to fight. We'd be wise to sneak away to the ships tonight, and quietly, before Hamet receives word of this treaty and before a civil war erupts."

And sneak away we did, like thieves in the night, a retreat not befitting a lowly band of robbers, much less our valiant army that had crossed the Sahara on foot and then prevailed against nearly impossible odds. Arriving in the Port of Lisbon, I rewarded each of my warriors with a generous pay bonus and a night of free drinks at one of the many wharfside pubs that my business partners and I owned. I then

retired to my country estate where I sipped
port wine in solitude, drinking late into the
night, hauntings from my past buzzing about the
room as I stared hatefully at the aging man who
was looking back at me in my den's mirror.

CHAPTER 18
Napoleon the Conqueror

October 1807: The pompously overdressed royal courier rapt on my villa's front door with the frenetic agitation of an asylum lunatic, demanding my presence with his ringing voice, demanding so loudly that the commotion whipped my guard dogs into a howling frenzy. I lighted my bedside candle and then stepped carefully downstairs to answer him, now regretting my decision to fire my latest butler, a man that I had been compelled to release for his inability to get along with my beloved bulldogs, pets that I had imported at great expense from Britain on a blockade runner right under the noses of the French naval blockade. Irritable, as old men tend to be in the wee hours, I threw open my door and greeted the surprised courier with the mouth of my pistol.

"Don't shoot! I apologize for awakening you but I bear an urgent message from His Majesty, Principe Joao, who demands your immediate presence." Said the velvet-clad messenger in perfectly enunciated English.

"Damnation man, does the prince have any idea what time it is! I pray that this is a matter of life-or-death, for it may become one if I find that my royal friend has awakened me for a frivolous matter! I said, half-jokingly.

"Principe Joao did not inform me of the purpose of my errand, Sir, but his instructions are quite clear and the air about the court suggests that the prince is burdened with a heavy concern."

I dressed quickly in my finest clothes, for though young in age, the ruler of Portugal, Principe Joao, was a serious man who demanded courtesy from his subjects. Principe Joao had

ruled as regent in place of his mother, Regina
Marie I, ever since the beloved queen had
suffered a nervous breakdown after receiving
the news of the execution of the French Royal
Family during that country's tumultuous
revolution. As I rode alongside the prince's
courier, I laughed at the irony that fate had
chosen to rescue me from King Taaksin's Siam
only to find me in yet another kingdom that
suffered from an insane monarch. At least
Principe Joao was an able man, I thought, a
blessing to a country that might have gone the
way of France were it in the hands of a less
capable leader.

Riding briskly through the countryside
and then through the lamp lit boulevards of
Lisbon's government district, the prince's
messenger and I arrived at Queluz Palace
shortly after 3:00 AM, the moon shining
brightly overhead in the starry sky. Grim
appearing musketmen waved us through the
palace's gate and then whisked us into the
throne room, a throne room which contained bold
displays of all manner of artifacts from
Portugal's South American, African, and East
Asian colonies in addition to the most prized
artifact: a shiny-red brazilwood table with
Prince Henry the Navigator's sextant perched
proudly atop. Our presence was announced by the
quivering courier who bowed deeply to Principe
Joao, the prince seated on his gilded,
brazilwood throne, presently lost in debate
with a crowded entourage of government
ministers. The prince waved me forward, his
face plastered with a foul grimace, his eyes
sunken and telling of a man who was straining
under the pressure of a great dilemma.

"Good morning, Mr. Lee." Principe Joao began in
English, a courtesy that he frequently offered
me though I spoke the Portuguese tongue
fluently. The prince was an accomplished
linguist, fluent in four European tongues and

boasting a basic command of another half dozen, including a smattering of exotic languages from his African and American colonies. His English was a work in progress, however, and was still spoken with a heavy accent. "I regret having wake you this early," the prince continued, "but the French have had deliver an…how do you say…ultimatum. I believe this word is correct. Napoleon, that scoundrel, that evil man, require that I accept his 'Continental System' within one week or he will invade to remove me off my throne. Even now, one hundred thousand French is in Spain, prepare for invasion."

In 1806, the warmongering Emperor of France, Napoleon Bonaparte—basking in his victories against the Prussians, the Austrians, and the Venetians—had declared the ports of Europe closed to the ships of his archenemy, the British Empire, a blockade that was known as the Continental System. Only two countries had dared to oppose the French despot, The Kingdom of Sweden and The Kingdom of Portugal, both close allies of the British crown. In response to this Portuguese defiance, Empereur Napoleon had quietly moved a hundred thousand battle-hardened soldiers into the territories of his Spanish ally, planning to conquer Portugal by force of arms if Principe Joao refused to bow to what would be Napoleon's final ultimatum.

"You are military man, man of the much experience, and I need very much your advice for this problem. I wish to fight—very, very much I wish—but British cannot help us, they is still too weak and too afraid for fight Napoleon on land. King George III, he remember still his many defeat while try to fight Napoleon army on land." The prince continued, his face filled with hopeless despair.

"My Lord, I am honored to serve you. I am well informed of the state of your armies for I work

closely with your generals. Indeed, I am
honored to call many of these brave men my
friends. It is with the greatest reluctance
that I must inform you that our armies stand no
chance of defeating Napoleon. Your generals are
afraid to tell you this, but you must know that
fighting the French in our current state will
only bring destruction to Portugal. I implore
Your Majesty to bow to the tyrant's demands and
to bide our time until the British can more
fully support us." I said forcefully, fully
aware that I was the only voice of reason in a
room full of timid bureaucrats.

"Dees is treachery!" One of the prince's
English-speaking civil advisors boomed from
across the room, the rest of the monarch's
delegation silent for none of them spoke a word
of my native tongue.

"Calm yourself, Royler, we will no accomplish
anything by fight each other." Principe Joao
gently chided as the room fell silent once
more.

"Your Majesty, there is another option that you
may not have considered." I said, switching to
Portuguese to include the entire room in our
conversation. "Though our land forces are weak,
our navy remains powerful. Undoubtedly, one of
Napoleon's aims is to commandeer our fleet for
use in his planned invasion of Britain. We
could deprive Napoleon of both of his
objectives, deposing our monarchy and capturing
our fleet, by fleeing the Portuguese mainland
and establishing a new capital in the Colony of
Brazil."

        Principe Joao nodded thoughtfully with
his hand on his chin and then waved me away as
he and his ministers retired to a private
conference room for further debate. I returned
to my villa a shaken and disheartened man,
fearful for both my own and my adopted

country's futures. If Napoleon captured France, what fate would befall me, a wealthy and landed American, I wondered as I poured myself a stiff glass of brandy, brandy made from wines grown on my private vineyard. Nothing good, I rapidly concluded. The United States had failed to support the French Revolution, a decision that the French unanimously regarded as treachery. The French opinion of the Americans had not been improved by the terms of the Louisiana Purchase four years ago, a land deal during which the United States had paid a paltry sum of fifteen million dollars in exchange for all of the French territories drained by the Mississippi River, an offer that the cash-strapped Empereur Napoleon had been forced to accept due to his enormous war debts.

November 1807: Swww…BOOM! The French invasion forces poured from their field camps in The Kingdom of Spain across the Portuguese borders like a plague of locusts feasting on a ripe harvest. I stood with my mercenaries on our training field, my men aligned in a disciplined formation as we listened to the foreboding sound of the French artillery thudding in the distance.

"They can't be far away now, the cannon fire grows louder!" Dr. Watkins whispered into my ear. "Shall we march to defend one of the mountain passes? If we make at double-time we might yet beat the French to the Gracie Pass where we could fight a delaying action in the narrows."

"No, we'll wait for our runner to return, there's no point in risking the lives of our men fighting for a hopeless cause. If Principe Joao requests our assistance, then we'll gladly oblige him; otherwise, we stand fast." I responded. Though I was as eager to fight Napoleon as my dear friend, I had long since

reconciled myself to the reality that this was
a war that could not be won.

"Speak of the devil." Dr. Watkins said as our
runner galloped up on his war mount.

"Sir, Principe Joao sends a message." The
runner reported as his horse skidded in front
of us.

"Out with it!" I commanded as I waved for Helio
Macellaro, who had been supervising the
soldiers as they cleaned their muskets for the
third time today.

"Sir, Principe Joao requests your immediate
presence at Queluz Palace." The runner said
with a look of worry on his fright-paled face.

"For what, damn it! Napoleon's forces are less
than a day's march from Lisbon! What we need
are marching orders, not councils!"

"The prince did not give an explanation but the
palace is in a great uproar."

        I shook my head in frustration as Helio,
Dr. Watkins, and I beckoned our horses. We rode
off towards the palace, riding as quickly as an
Atlantic tempest whips onto the Portuguese
shores. Before departing, I had instructed my
men to pack their belongings and to flee to
their homes if I had not returned within two
hours. The doctor, Helio, and I found the
streets of Lisbon to be in a state of great
panic with disgraceful looting and rioting
filling the boulevards as the greatly
outnumbered garrison soldiers stood by
impotently, merely observing the chaos. My
comrades and I reached Queluz Palace panting
from our hurried ride. At the palace we found
hundreds of noblemen with their servants
carrying all manner of items in their arms and
on their backs, items ranging from priceless

artifacts to utilitarian furniture, carried out of the palace and onto a train of horse-drawn wagons. They appeared to be working to empty the palace as busily as honeybees buzz about a rose garden, even the children having been put to work. I stopped a trembling princess, a charming young girl of twelve years with whom I had made an acquaintance during my frequent courtesy visits to the palace. I implored her to tell me where I might find Principe Joao. The terrified child pointed in the direction of the throne room, a throne room in which I found defeated appearing ministers huddled about their prince, the smell of fear hanging thickly in the air.

"Mr. Lee, I thank God that you have make it here safe." The prince said through a forced smile. "I have decide that you are right…I…I will flee to Brazil." The monarch said as he fought back his tears. "I have order the fleet, order many weeks ago, to return to Lisbon. The spies of Napoleon know this…they think I not know of the plan to attack us from Spain…that I was fear of attack from the sea instead. I do this on purpose, position my army to guard the coast with very few of my men in the garrisons by Spain. I have trick Napoleon and he do not know that my real plan is escape. For days I have been load my ships with the treasure of my kingdom. What you see now, this chaos, is only the last minute packing, the tip of the iceberg as the English say. I will flee tonight and I ask you to come with me to help rebuild my kingdom in Brazil."

I bowed to the prince as I replied, "I am honored, Your Majesty, and I will serve the ruler of my adopted home with all of my energies."

There was no time for my companions and I to return to our homes and we were forced to flee fair Portugal, the land that had been so kind to us, with only the clothes on our backs. Dr. Watkins and I were hustled down to the wharfs by the Prince's royal guard. In the great Port of Lisbon we found quarter awaiting us aboard the prince's frigate, *Vasco da Gama*, a finely constructed vessel which was so overloaded with royal cargo that it sat dangerously low in the water, so low in fact that the ship's captain was compelled to abandon twenty of his vessel's forty cannon onto the docks to ensure that the *Vasco da Gama* was seaworthy. As we settled into our quarters, Helio was suddenly overcome by emotion.

"I can't go with you, Jonathan. I love you as a brother but I cannot abandon my country to the French. I must stay and fight! I will return to the regiment and lead them into battle!"

I attempted to argue with him but to no avail. I embraced my valiant friend and wished him well. Then I boarded the *Vasco da Gama* and began the second voyage of my life across the Atlantic.

CHAPTER 19:
Colonia do Brasil

January 1808: Principe Joao's fleet of twenty-five frigates and an equal number of merchantmen cast off from Lisbon Harbor only hours before Napoleon's cavalry spearheaded into the wealth-and-artifact stripped city. Ten thousand of Portugal's finest citizens, and nearly as many of the kingdom's sailors, voyaged across the stormy Atlantic in ships that were filled to the brim with cargos and luggage, so weighted down that a two month long routine voyage was transformed into a three month long ordeal. Sea weary and overcome with melancholy remorse for the plight of fair Portugal, the Prince's entourage, Dr. Watkins, and I finally spotted the coastline of our new home: the wild and enormous Colonia do Brasil.

Granted to the Portuguese crown by the Roman Pope's Treaty of Tordesillas[29] in 1494, Brazil was named after the colony's first profitable export, brazilwood, a deciduous tree that yields an orange-red wood that is highly prized in the construction of fine musical instruments and exquisite furniture. The early Portuguese colonists soon discovered that the climate of their new domain was ideal for growing sugarcane, the plant from which table sugar is derived, and they had transformed the

---

29. Treaty of Tordesillas: A treaty between Portugal and Spain, decreed by the Pope in 1494 to settle the two Catholic nations' territorial disputes in the recently discovered New World. The treaty essentially consisted of a longitudinal line that was hand drawn on a map by Pope Alexander VI, a line that arbitrarily divided the newly discovered Americas. Only later was it learnt, through further exploration, that all of the New World, save for Brazil, lay within the Spanish half of the divide. This is why Spanish is the spoken language in all of the Central and South American colonies, save for Brazil, where Portuguese is the spoken tongue.

untamed colony into the world's largest
producer of this lucrative commodity. More
recently, the Brazilian colonists had
discovered rich alluvial deposits of gold.
River panning for this precious resource had
become an important industry and an important
source of wealth for the Portuguese crown. But
all was not well in the prosperous colony.
Popular revolts in 1792 and 1798 had been
brutally suppressed by Principe Joao's regime,
the leaders of the democratic-populist revolt
hanged and quartered, their body parts
distributed throughout the colony as a warning
to those who would dare to defy their monarch.

  As the capital of Brazil, Rio de Janeiro,
neared into sight I was struck by the modern
European design of the city. Like a miniature
Lisbon, Rio de Janeiro was filled with Iberian
architecture that was painted in the bright
pinks, yellows, and aqua blues that the
Portuguese adore, the buildings topped by
orange-tiled roofs with Catholic crosses
reaching skyward from their pinnacles. The city
streets were wide boulevards that were divided
down their centers with yellow-and-red
flowering brazilwood trees, every building
constructed with tall, wide windows to provide
the inhabitants with adequate ventilation
during the sweltering Brazilian summers, the
peak of which was in January in the Southern
Hemisphere.

June 1808: Principe Joao and his wife, the
devious Spanish Princesa Carolota Joaquina, set
up their court in the middle of Rio de Janeiro
at the Paco Imperial, a large tri-pronged
building with a rectangular center and two
shorter triangular roofed divisions on either
side, both connected directly to the building's
center. Though lacking the historical grandeur
of Queluz Palace, the Paco Imperial was a
finely constructed white- and-gray building
with ornately welded iron balconies. The

building was dressed in carefully sculpted
stone facades, stone facades that made the
building both beautiful and imposing, both
lovely and fear-inspiring. Principe Joao found
himself pleased with his new capital city but
his ever-plotting wife did not share in the
prince's optimistic appraisal. Personally, I
found Rio de Janeiro to be a surprisingly
comfortable city and I did not regret my
decision to accompany the prince on his voyage,
a sentiment that was supported by news that
arrived from Portugal a week after we had
disembarked from our voyage, news that detailed
the brutality of the French occupation under
Napoleon's commander, General Junot.

It was now June, the middle of Brazil's
mild winter, and I sat with Principe Joao in
his library flanked by the monarch's domestic
advisors who were debating the prince's
proposal to sign into law a bill that would
abolish the tributary status of Brazil to the
mother country. As we argued, a courier with
clothes still smelling of sea salt approached
us with a satchel of news documents and
official correspondences. The reports from
Portugal were not heartening: General Junot was
ruthlessly suppressing the rebellious populace,
hanging Portuguese rebels in the streets of
Lisbon from the city's famous lampposts. To the
east, Napoleon had betrayed his Spanish allies
and overthrown King Charles IV, placing the
Spanish crown onto the head of his imbecile
brother, Joseph Bonaparte. In the messenger's
satchel, alongside the dreary news from home,
was a diplomatic communiqué from the British, a
communiqué that I could clearly see stoked
Prince Joao's spirits as he eyes tracked down
it. The ministers and I sat silently, our eyes
burning at the back of the British document
with the greatest of curiosities, neither the
ministers not I able to muster the courage to
ask the prince what it said. After a good
while, Principe Joao laid the communiqué flat

for all to see, a look of concern now across his face.

"Dee British wish land an army in Portugal." The prince said to me in English, his Portuguese-speaking ministers glaring in my direction, full of animosity for being cut out of the conversation. "I ask your advice because you know military matters of war very well, Mr. Lee."

"I'm honored, Your Majesty." I replied, bowing my head as I spoke. "This proposal is a double-edged blade: if we refuse the British request, then the French will consolidate their rule over Portugal. Yet if we accede to British military intervention, Portugal will become a battlefield like Austria, Denmark, Prussia, and Italy before it. It is thus with the greatest reluctance that I advise you to allow the British to land their troops and to order the legislators of the Cortes Constitucionais Portuguesas to support the British in whatever way possible. It is better to fight and to lose than to surrender to Napoleon! We fled Portugal because there was no chance of victory, but the British now give us a fighting chance and we should take it!"

The prince nodded then stood and turned his back to the ministers and I, his hands clasped behind him, his head bent deep in thought. The prince stared out of the library's window onto the sun-kissed braziltree and rosebush lined boulevard that lay below us, lazily meandering past the Paco Imperial in its journey to the harbor. The prince stared into the distance, the weight of decision pressing heavily on his shoulders as the ministers and I sat silently in anticipation. Finally, Principe Joao spun around and announced to his delegation in Portuguese: "Send a message to the British that Portugal is prepared for war and that King George III's army is most welcome in my domain." The ministers stood quickly, eager to begin their task, but the prince motioned for them to remain seated. "I have already made one monumental decision today and I see no need to stop at only one. From henceforth, Brazil will trade openly with the world," the prince stated as his ministers stared at him in disbelief.

I had no doubt that this declaration, the end of Portuguese mercantilism in her colonies, would win the Brazilian populace over to their prince, Brazilian's who had thus far given the young monarch a lukewarm welcome. I also had no doubt that this was Principe Joao's primary motivation for the decree for he was an astute politician with a keen ear for the pulse of his subjects. For three hundred years, Brazil had restricted to trading only with its mother country, Portugal, and the Portuguese monarch's decree would open the world markets to Brazil's plethora of valuable exports. As revolutionary an idea as this was, Principe Joao went even further. "Furthermore, from henceforth the Kingdom of Portugal will be known as the United Kingdom of Portugal, Brazil, and the Algarves[30]." The jaws of the Portuguese ministers dropped but I was not surprised. It was a smart move, I thought, clever politics because declaring Brazil a co-equal to Portugal would entitle the former colony to representation in the Cortes. Upon receipt of word of the trade agreement, an action that was sure to enrage the Old World Portuguese, the Brazilian's would become the prince's strongest supporters and he would be able to manipulate the new Brazilian representatives in the Cortes to do his bidding. The ministers and I were dismissed. As I exited the library, I noticed

30. Algarves: The southernmost provinces of Portugal. Historically, an area with a higher concentration of persons of the Muslim faith and of Moor background.

that the prince's wife, Princessa Carolota
Joaquina, had been silently eavesdropping on
our meeting from the adjacent lounge and was
now stalking over to her husband, instigating a
heated argument.

As I had been instructed by the prince, I
waited for him outside in the sculpture crowded
hallway, meandering amongst the priceless
Portuguese artworks, some still in their
packings from the voyage, as I waited to join
the prince on a tour of the Brazilian
countryside. As I listened to the royal couple
banter like two wild dogs fighting over a deer
leg, I marveled at the quantity of the
unrivalled works of Renaissance work that had
accompanied us from Queluz Palace clear across
the stormy sea to find a new home in the
hallway of a building in what had, until the
prince's arrival, been a remote and backwards
colony and that was now, due to the prince's
intervention, an equal partner in one of
Europe's oldest dynastic empires. I was forced
to endure fifteen minutes of ceaseless arguing,
bickering that pierced through the library's
thick brazilwood door and rang through the
stone hallways, a ceaseless chorus of the
princess' hate-filled, soprano soliloquy,
shouting obscenities at her defenseless
husband, words that would have made my soul
cringe were they to have sprung forth from a
prostitute's mouth and that I simply could not
fathom coming from the petite lips of a well-
bred Spanish princess. I jumped, startled, as I
heard the sound of a vase shattering that was
followed by a cry of pain from Principe Joao,
who fled into the hallway holding a
handkerchief to his bleeding forehead.

"My Lord, are you alright?" I implored as I ran
over to him.

"I think I will live," he said with a smirk.
"Let us go the tour of Brazil now, I cannot

stay here more longer with this crazy bitch."
Principe Joao muttered in English as he pointed
scornfully at the screaming Princesa Joaquina,
who was busily throwing the royal library's
books off of the shelves and onto the floor.

Switching back to Portuguese, Principe Joao
ordered his guards to escort the princess
wherever she traveled and not to let her out of
their sight for any reason. I then followed the
prince to the royal carriage that stood waiting
for us. We rode off accompanied by a troop of
royal guards, guards dressed in the purple and
white uniforms of their home, trotting away
towards the gold and diamond mining region of
Minas Gerais.

"My wife, she Spanish and she have always love
Spain more than she love me…or our children. In
Europe, I must watch her always because she
would like much to see Spanish man on my
throne. It sadden me much to know this, but it
is true. Now my wife, she far from the Spain
that she love and she make it known to all that
she do not think it right for royal princess to
live in New World…it is, how you say, beneath
her. So I must watch her more now than even in
the past," the prince shook his still oozing
head in sorrow, "but we shall not let her ruin
our great expedition. I have come to love this
Brazil, such a beautiful land!"

"Indeed it is beautiful, Your Majesty, and I am
grateful for the invitation to tour your realm
in such esteemed company."

Traveling out of Rio de Janeiro on the
muddy roads that led for three hundred miles to
Minas Gerais, the prince and I gawked
awestricken at the sight of parrots, toucans,
armadillos, and leopards that populated the
thickly forested countryside in such great
quantities that one could hardly travel for a
mile without spotting a new kind of exotic

animal. Our carriage crossed rickety bridges
over clear watered rivers, rivers that were
clogged with crocodiles as large as bulls,
crocodiles that looked as if they could easily
make a meal out of our carriage—horses and all.
The chattering forests were interrupted only by
sugarcane plantations and the prince and I
stopped to bed and dine at one of these
profitable enterprises, learning much of the
sugarcane business from the plantation master
as we broke bread at his table.

    The Brazilian plantations were run much
like the cotton fields in my native Virginia,
relying on African slaves for labor, work that
was backbreaking for the sugarcane plants often
grew to a height several heads higher than a
man is tall, with thick, hard stalks which were
felled with swipes from a razor-sharp reaper
and then ground into powder in a hand-cranked
mill. Table sugar was produced from the ground
sugarcane on the plantation itself, so that by
the time the crop was sold it was ready to go
straight to the market. The work was dangerous
for the sugarcane fields were filled with
dangerous brown snakes, called jararaca, and
deadly banana spiders: a large, light brown
creature that rears back onto its hind legs
before striking with a poison that is so potent
as to make death inevitable for any soul
unlucky enough to be bitten. Needless to say,
the unfortunate plantation slaves often
attempted escape, a chronic threat to the
plantation owners' purses. To counter against
escapes, and also against outright revolts, the
plantation owners employed heavily armed
overseers and vicious Brasileiro hounds to
maintain order in the fields. Another purpose
of these formidable defenses was to protect the
plantation against Indian attacks, which
occurred occasionally, perpetrated by natives
who lived hidden deep in the dark recesses of
the surrounding jungles. Any slave lucky enough
to slip through the plantation's perimeter

found himself alone in a deadly rain forest, his only hope of survival being to locate a quilombo, a term used by the Brazilian's to refer to the scattered communities of escaped slaves who lived side-by-side with the aboriginal natives in communities hidden away in the depths of the Amazon.

As we prepared to continue our journey, the plantation owner gifted a large bottle of Brazilian liquor to his prince, a bottle which Principe Joao and I gladly shared as we rode north on the muddy, country trails. The liquor was derived from sugarcane and called cachaca by the locals. It was light in complexion and went down smoothly, not unlike a high quality whiskey, though its appearance was more akin to that of golden rum. Traveling thirty miles per day, a trek made far more enjoyable by the cachaca, Prince Joao and I arrived at Vila Rica in the Minas Gerais province two weeks after we had begun our meandering journey. Vila Rica was of utilitarian construct with a neat, but simple, administrative center that sat high on a rocky hilltop. Workers shacks sat lined in orderly rows down the hillsides, surrounded by gold-panning streams and diamond mines. The diamond mines were burrowed into the earth in such great numbers that their runoff made the streams run thick with silt, an unfortunate occurrence for the gold-panners as filtering through the silt made their work exponentially more tedious, so much more tedious that the issue had led to bloodshed between the mining factions on more than one occasion. The prince and I made our way through the muddy streets of Vila Rica to the governor's estate, a large wooden house that stood proudly atop the pinnacle of the tallest hilltop, commanding an overview of the mines, rivers, and the forest below. We were warmly welcomed and provided with comfortable accommodations and a hearty welcoming feast by the royal governor, a man who seemed awestricken in the presence of royalty, hankering to his prince as a teenage boy panders to a beautiful woman. After the feast, the prince and I retired to the governor's balcony where we could speak in private, away from the ears of our host.

"I am tired from this journey, but I am glad to have…how you say…time to clear my mind of many troubles. I feel relax now and I have learn much about my new country, which I think has very much promise of the future." Said Principe Joao as we sipped cachaca and chomped on tan-brown brazilnuts, a pleasing little legume that is native to Brazil and that is a favorite snack of both the colonists and the slaves alike.

"I needed the holiday as much as you, My Lord. Dr. Watkins and I have been working like madmen in our endeavor to purchase land that is suitable for a vineyard, alas to no avail. The good doctor is also practicing medicine again, there being a severe shortage of physicians in Rio de Janeiro, and we are both eagerly awaiting word from Helio Macellaro on the fate of our mercenary regiment."

"I will help you find this land, do not worry about this. If we cannot find good land for the grapes, we will buy much wine from the Spanish colony in Chile where many wines of good taste come from. We no will have thirst, do not worry!" The prince said with a smile, his mood greatly improved since the start of our trek, a time when he had been in the depths of melancholy for several days as he had brooded over his marital entanglement. "Ah yes, I love Brazil much but I miss my country also, also very much. Do you miss yours, Jonathan?" Principe Joao asked, catching me off guard for I had buried my longings for Virginia deep in my soul years and years ago, determined not to let fruitless yearnings for my boyhood past to countermine my ability to enjoy the present.

Yet, though I was loath to admit it, I had silently suffered from a great homesickness for decades, a homesickness that had weighed heavily on my soul and that had been alleviated only partially by my entrepreneurial successes.

"I have longed for Virginia ever since I was forced to leave her as a young man, a young man who was barely old enough to grow whiskers on his wrinkleless face. It's been nearly thirty years since I've seen my brothers. I would especially like to see my brother, Henry, again one day for he and I did not part on favorable terms and I should like very much to make amends with him in person."

"Perhaps that day have come. I have been think much, think much on Portugal and how to save my kingdom from this Napoleon scoundrel. I should like for you go to Portugal and give me report on situation that is there. After, I think, I like for you to be my ambassador to United States. This new city, what it called…"

"Washington City, My Lord."

"Yes, to Washington City I send you with message that Brazil is open for trade and that I hope American's will join Brazil in New World alliance against Napoleon…alliance of trade and, I think, perhaps alliance of military too."

"I would be greatly honored to represent you, Your Majesty." I said with a smile, my heart lighter than it had been in decades at the prospect of seeing my home again.

CHAPTER 20:
At Long Last — Home

September 1808: Lisbon, Portugal. I wished Dr. Watkins well in his new medical practice, which he seemed to be thoroughly enjoying after a long respite from the profession. I boarded the command ship in one of the prince's three frigate strong communication fleets and, after a two month voyage across a rambunctious Atlantic, I was shocked to find the red-crested white flag of the Portuguese Empire fluttering above Lisbon Harbor. Purple and white uniformed Portuguese soldiers patrolled Lisbon's sunny boulevards, not a Frenchman in sight. I disembarked my frigate and then commanded the nearest Portuguese soldier to take me to his superiors. I was rapidly ferried from headquarters to higher headquarters until finally arriving in a military encampment that lay not far from my former villa, where I was to be introduced to the heroes who had liberated my adopted country only weeks before my arrival. I waited for several hours in the joint Portuguese-British command tent where my hosts provided me with a warm meal and a glass of British-Indian tea, a rare luxury since the commencement of Napoleon's wars nearly a decade prior. Tired from my long voyage, a voyage in which my escorts had been entangled in two skirmishes with prowling French frigates, I was beginning to nod off to sleep when an impeccably dressed, stone-faced British officer—his hair almost as red as his uniform, his skin as fair as a dove's feathers, save for his rosy cheeks—stormed into the command tent. The tent's battle captain jolted out of his chair and barked, "Atten-tion", as every man in the tent immediately dropped whatever he had been doing to stand at a stiff position-of-attention.

"Carry-on." The British officer muttered in reply as he stuck out his hand to greet me, asking me if I spoke any English, and upon recognizing that I was fluent, smiled and continued to speak. "I am Lieutenant-General Sir Arthur Wellesley of His Majesty King George III's Royal Expeditionary Force. My commanding officers, General Dalryple and General Burrard, are regrettably unavailable as they are currently reviewing the northern defenses that surround the city of Porto with your army's commander, General Bernardino Freire. However, I believe that I can answer your questions to the prince's satisfaction."

"Please inform me the current military situation, I have been at sea for two months and I had expected to land in a country that was infested with Frenchmen."

"You are undoubtedly pleasantly surprised. I made landfall with my army in early August and we were soon joined by droves of Portuguese soldiers, soldiers whom the French had employed as domestic police but who immediately defected to our cause in great numbers. The French attacked us at Vimeiro but our lines held and our subsequent counterattack succeeded in driving Junot's forces into disarray. Alas, against my protestations, my superior officers elected not to pursue the French formations. Several days later they signed The Convention of Sintra, allowing Junot's army to return to France unmolested."

"My god, why?" I exclaimed, shocked to my core.

"As I said, against my protestations, protestations given so strongly that I was nearly relieved of my command by General Burrard. King George is not pleased, and rightfully so. I am ordered to accompany my commanders on the next British fleet to report to the king in person and to explain to him why we let Junot slip away. I fear that my career is ruined, but that is my concern and not yours. You may report to Principe Joao that Portugal is secure, for the moment anyhow, and that his commanding generals, General Forjaz and General Freire, are hard at work rebuilding the Portuguese Army and that they are making steady progress."

I thanked Sir Wellesley[31] for his report and I wished him well, sincerely hoping that King George III would spare him of punishment for his superior officer's epical failure of military judgment. Sir Wellesley struck me as an exceptionally competent officer with the heart of a lion and I thought it unfortunate that his commanders were not from the same stock. I found my villa as I had left it, save for a note from Helio Macellaro that I found lying on my dinner table. I read the crumpled little note with tears in my eyes for I had learnt at the allied headquarters that Helio, and most of my mercenary regiment, had fallen while fighting a heroic defense of Porto in 1807.

31. Known later in life as The Duke of Wellington.

Dear Jonathan,

If you find this letter before my return, I trust that your sea voyage was safe and I hope that you have returned of sound mind and body. I have led our regiment to aid the defense of Porto, where a commander by the name of Freire intends to make a stand, unlike the cowardly commanders in the south who have collectively surrendered to the French tyrant's heathen hordes. The men are in good spirits and are eager for a fight. I intend to make a good show in the battles of the north, regardless of the odds that stand against us, and I pray that the men and I will bring honor to our company's good name, as we have always done in the past.

Your Brother-In-Arms,
Helio Macellaro

I sat at my dinner table staring at the ghostly letter as the sun crept beneath the horizon and shone its last rays through the windowpane behind me, praying that the heavens would keep my dear friend's soul at peace. The crowing of a neighbor's rooster awoke me to the discovery that I had fallen asleep on top of Helio's letter; the excitement of returning to Portugal had been so exhilarating that I had not recognized my own exhaustion. I crisply folded Helio's letter and placed it into my breast pocket and then I made my way down to my wine cellar, where I was comforted to find my collection resting as I had left it. I popped open a dusty bottle of port wine and poured out a hearty glass, the stout wine calming my nerves enough to allow me to write my report to Principe Joao. Having completed my report and feeling somewhat refreshed from my wine, I blew out my candles and locked my villa's front door. Then I made my way to Lisbon Harbor where I delivered my report to the captain of a ship bound for Sao Paulo. I waited by the docks for the arrival of a ship that was heading for America, a wait that turned into a long respite of several weeks, thanks to Napoleon's blockade, which harassed even Yankee shipping. After nearly a month of bored anticipation, I was fortunate enough to find passage on a merchantman bound for New York City. I left Portugal for the last time, watching its shoreline fade over the horizon with great sadness.

December 1808: Oh Virginia, home at last! My stagecoach arrived at Leesylvania two days before Christmas and I was delighted to find that my brother Henry was home, having feared that he would be on holiday for Christmas Time. The bite of the American air was chill, but invigorating, a cold that I had not felt in decades and that my body welcomed despite my advancing age. Leesylvania stood almost as I remembered it and I broke into tears of joy as my stagecoach bounced and rattled up the carefully kept path that led past my family's winter-fallowed cotton fields to the Lee Family Manor. The coach pulled up to my mother's great wraparound porch and Henry ran out of the house to meet me, carrying a young boy in his arms.

"My god, I thought this day would never come!" Henry exclaimed as he gently set his boy down onto the porch and then engulfed me in a bearhug embrace. "Robert, this is your Uncle Jonathan, give him a hug! My wife and the other children are on holiday visiting her family but young Robert refuses to leave his Papa and he has compelled his poor mother to leave him here with me. Our brothers are off in Washington City, politicking as usual. The Christmas Season is a time of elite parties in the capital, parties full of Democratic-Republicans whose company I would prefer not to keep. So I agreed to stay to watch after the plantation, and I am now even gladder that I did!"

My brother, his child, and I slowly walked the grounds of our estate, pausing at the family cemetery where I solemnly gazed upon my parent's tomb as I whispered an inaudible apology for the grief that I knew that I had shackled them with in their final years. Henry and I traded tales as we strolled about the manor grounds, Henry informing me that his Federalist Party had just lost another Presidential Election, a political battle fought against the Democratic-Republicans who had propelled their man into the nation's highest office for the third consecutive election.

"This man, James Madison, newly elected to office, he will have a hard time refusing the warmongering of the Democratic-Republican electorate. The clamoring for war against Britain has grown so loud now that it is difficult to find a newspaper publisher who isn't a war-hawking Democratic-Republican stooge." My brother scornfully reported as he kicked a rock that landed some dozen yards ahead of us. "A friend of mine in Baltimore, Mr. Alexander Hanson, is planning to start a Federalist newspaper next month and I have agreed to provide him with the capital necessary to begin printing."

"Then I shall look for his newspaper with great eagerness when I am in Washington City."

"In Washington City?"

"I'm unfortunately only able to stay for a short visit. I'm currently employed by Principe Joao, the Regent of Portugal, as his ambassador to the United States of America. Principe Joao has decided to open Brazil to traders from all friendly nations, that is to say, to nations not allied with Napoleon." I could not bring myself to tell my brother the other half of my assignment, to convince the American President to enter the war on the side of Portugal and Britain. Regardless, based on my brother's opinions and my personal tasting of the American sentiments in the alehouses that I had dined at during my travel from New York City, the chance of the Americans entering the war on Principe Joao's side was remote at best. I had long since concluded that I would consider my diplomacy successful if I merely managed to keep America from allying itself with the French despot.

February 1809: Washington was a small city, built on drained swampland that abutted the Potomac River. Though the roads were finished, paved with carefully cut cobblestone, vast empty lots stood bare at nearly every intersection. Those city blocks that that were filled contained half-finished buildings, structures on which both slave and free workers toiled side-by-side, working even in the most inclement weather, such was the hurry to complete their nation's new capital. A few of the most important government edifices stood completed, built in Greco-Roman style and including The Capitol Building and the presidential mansion, The White House. In late January, I arrived just in the time to witness James Madison taking the oath of office as he was sworn in as the fourth President of the United States of America. Mr. Madison's predecessor, Thomas Jefferson, stood by the new president's side as Mr. Madison took his oath. I had met Mr. Jefferson, who was a distant relation of mine, when we were both young men in Virginia at a political dinner that my father had hosted to raise money for the Continental Army during the Revolution. I remembered Mr. Jefferson as an articulate and intelligent man with a great zeal for populist democracy.

I wandered over to Mr. Jefferson after the inauguration and I was pleased to discover that he recognized me, Mr. Jefferson saying, somewhat gruffly, that I bore a strong resemblance to my brother, Henry, as I approached him. This observation was somewhat uncomfortable for my Federalist brother and the Democratic-Republican Mr. Jefferson had become bitter political enemies. Nonetheless, when I explained my capacity as the ambassador from Portugal, Mr. Jefferson was kind enough to introduce me to President Madison, who I found to be an agreeable gentleman with an eloquent tongue and a sharp mind. Agreeable or not, it was clear to me that President Madison had no interest in entertaining the idea of an alliance against France, a subject on which he was so adamant that I dared not broach the issue again. My meeting in the empty White House was not entirely unsuccessful for Mr. Jefferson showed great interest in the prospect of importing Brazilian sugarcane and he even requested that I have Principe Joao send him a bottle of fine cachaco, Mr. Jefferson being a connoisseur of exotic liquors which he enjoyed serving at diplomatic dinners to visiting foreign dignitaries. I thanked President Madison and Mr. Jefferson for their time and then I retired to the office that I had rented in a nearly finished building to write my report to Principe Joao.

July 1812: Oh, terrible day! The post from Baltimore arrived announcing a most horrible event that had transpired in Baltimore. A week ago, Henry's good friend, Alexander Hanson, the editor of *The Federal Republican*, was attacked by a mob of Democratic-Republicans in his newspaper's office, an attack instigated by Mr. Hanson's opposition to the newly declared American war against Britain. My brother had

rushed to Mr. Hanson's aid and the two
Federalists had been scouting the city for a
new office in which to publish the
newspaper—the original office having been burnt
to the ground by the warmongers—when they were
assaulted by a Democratic-Republican lynch mob.
The paper said that Henry had suffered severe
wounds while putting up a spirited defense of
Mr. Hanson, who had escaped unharmed. I dropped
the paper and penned a quick letter of
resignation to Principe Joao. My mission to
keep America out of the global Napoleonic
conflict having failed anyway, and besides,
knowing that the fair-minded prince would
forgive my abandonment of my assigned duties in
favor of caring for my family during a time of
great need.

I rushed northwards from Washington City
to Baltimore, galloping across the summer-
roasted farm fields, fields still slippery from
the previous day's thundershowers, past farm
houses and cattle fields and into the State of
Mary Land. I found Henry resting at a local
Federalist doctor's house. My brother's wounds
were extensive, his face and scalp gashed from
the blows of a dozen horse whips, his abdomen
distended and with great purple bruises the
size of frying pans over both of his flanks.
Henry's speech was somewhat garbled; odd I had
thought, for his jaw was one of the few places
that his body had not sustained severe damage.
I would later learn from the kindly old doctor
that the change in Henry's voice was secondary
to blows he had suffered to his cranium, a
condition from which my poor brother would
never fully recover.

After several weeks of indulging in the
physician's restful hospitality, I accompanied
Henry to Leesylvania where two of our other
brothers, Charles—an attorney, and Richard—the
primary administrator of our plantation, met us
and cried tears of joyful sadness at our safe

return and at Henry's pathetic appearance. I
explained to my family that Henry's physician
had recommended that he take a sabbatical to
the islands of the Caribbean, the wise
physician believing that the clean and sunny
air might aid Henry's recovery. Henry and I bid
farewell to our loving family and we purchased
passage aboard a rum trading schooner destined
for the Caribbean island of Jamaica, my family
praying for Henry's recovery and wishing us
tearful farewells.

AFTERWARD:

I have elected to leave this manuscript in the care of Mrs. Henry Lee III, aka: Anne Hill Carter, and I hope that she will share it with her young boy, Robert, when he is of age if, heaven forbid, fate sees to it that Henry and I do not return from our voyage. Robert is a precocious boy and he is already beginning to show an intense obsession with all things military, undoubtedly a trait that he has inherited from his father and, perhaps, from his Uncle Jonathan as well. I hope that the narratives found in this journal will dissuade the young lad from continuing our family's military tradition, a tradition which I would just as well see evaporate into the sky as rain clouds do in the summer heat. Waiting for our carriage to the wharfs where our ship is awaiting, I watch young Robert chasing his older brothers with a toy sword that he has fashioned from a sugarcane pole; I must confess that I am not optimistic about the prospects of my little book accomplishing its goal.

Ne Incautus Futuri,
Jonathan E. Lee

About the Author
By: Leonardo Antony Noto

Greetings! I am a military physician who writes under the *nom de plume* — Leonardo Antony Noto. *The Life of a Colonial Fugitive* is my first novel, a work of love that was three years in the making. In my day job, the one that pays the bills, I am currently a general practitioner but I will be beginning a psychiatric residency at the end of the year when I have completed my military commitment. This novel was borne out of my lifelong passion for military history and my relatively recent enthusiasm for the sport of muay Thai, which I have practiced for four years, having taken up the sport during my third year of medical school as a way to exhale stress! I have five other works in various stages of completion including: a medical-science thriller entitled *The Cannabinoid Hypothesis*, a historical fiction thriller entitled *Venetian Seas*, a novel exploring street gangs entitled *Lords and Disciples*, and a two-part memoir entitled *Intrusive Memory* and *Three Years in the Army*. I hope that you have enjoyed reading *The Life of a Colonial Fugitive* as much as I have enjoyed writing it and I hope to see you again in the near future!

Special thanks to: Mike Cole, M.D., Marshal Blanks, Carol McRae, Cheryl Helbing, Heidi Helbing, and LTC(R) Steve Noble for their unending support of both my medical career and my writing.

~Author

REFERENCES

1. Axelrod, A. (2007). *The Real History of the American Revolution: A New Look at the Past.* Sterling Publishing Co., Inc.- A highly accessible, and highly entertaining, glimpse into the birth of America.

2. *The History Place: American Revolution.* (1998).http://historyplace.com/unitedstates/revolution/revwar-77.htm. - The best Revolutionary War timeline that I've ever come across.

3. *Liberty or Death.* (1993). KOEI Co., Ltd. -My favorite childhood videogame and a large part of what inspired me to write this book.

4. *Henry Lee III- "Light Horse Harry".* http://www.nps.gov/history/museum/exhibits/arho/FamilyTree.html

5. *Henry Lee II.* http://en.wikipedia.org/wiki/Henry_Lee_II - I'm a big fan of Wikipedia and I use it frequently. However, I always double check any information that I find there (sometimes I triple check it) and I'd recommend that you do the same.

6. *Henry Lee III.* http://en.wikipedia.org/wiki/Henry_Lee_III

7. Washington, DC to Cherry Valley, NY. http://maps.google.com/maps?f=d&source=s_d&saddr=Washington,... - I use Google Maps extensively in my research and I am a huge fan of their excellent search engine. I also used Google's translator service several times while writing this novel.

8. *Quebec City.* http://en.wikipedia.org/wiki/Quebec_City

9. Geiser, K. (1869). *Redemptions and Indentured Servants in the Colony and Commonwealth of Pennsylvania*. Nabu Press (Oct. 14, 2010). – An aged book that I used to confirm the cost of travel across the Atlantic in the 18th century.

10. http://www.bignell.uk.com. – A website that I found useful for determining the cost of trans-Atlantic passage at the end of the 18th century.

11. King, J. and Wilkinson, J. (2001). *Portugal: Moonshine, Markets and Manueline Marvels*. Lonely Planet Publications. – A solidly written series of travel guides with colorful pictures and strong historical facts presented in a fun-to-read manner.

12. Anderson, J. (2000). *The History of Portugal*. Greenwood Press. – A textbook that I used to confirm and/or elaborate on information on Portugal that I initially obtained by web-browsing.

13. http://www.intowine.com/port.html - Information on portwine.

14. http://www.portugal.com/information/portwine - More information on portwine.

15. http://www.historyworld.net/wrldhis/PlainTextHistories.asp?groupid=1709&HistoryID=ab46&gtrack=pthc – Information on the Portuguese monarchy.

16. www.britannica.com – Basic information on Queen Maria 1st

17. www.lisbon-guide.com – Good source of basic information on Lisbon.

18. *Kasteel de Goede Hoop.*
http://en.wikipedia.org

19. Baker, C. and Phongpaichit, P. (2008). *A History of Thailand.* Cambridge University Press. – A well-written overview of Thai history. Fairly readable, although those with an interest in the history and politics of Southeast Asia will find this title significantly more entertaining than the average reader.

20. Boraas, Tracey. (2003). *Countries and Cultures: Thailand.* Bridgestone Books. – A short, but highly useful, overview of Thailand including the country's history, geography, contemporary politics, etc. Easily read in twenty minutes but, nonetheless, highly informative.

21. http://www.answers.com/topic/1767- A well-designed website that is very useful for its historical timelines.

22. http://www.answers.com/topic/1782.

23. *Muay Thai.*
http://en.wikipedia.org/wiki/Muay_Thai

24. Kru Bryan Dobler. *Dobler's Double-Dose Muay Thai.*- My muay Thai instructor in Fontana, CA. In addition to teaching muay Thai, Kru Dobler also teaches muay Boran weapons techniques.

25. Stephens, J. (1997). *Weird History 101.* Adams Media, an F+W Publications Company. -As its title would suggest, this book is a bit on the strange side. Cleverly written, Mr. Stephen's takes primary historical sources and weaves them into an entertaining behind-the-scenes look at history.

26. Simmons, D. (2011). *Early Navy Commandos Buried in Tripoli.* Stars and Stripes, Vol 9,

No. 58 -The newspaper supplied to American forces, free of charge, who are deployed overseas. I ran across this article while finishing up this novel during my deployment in Iraq and the final chapters of Jonathan E. Lee's life were born.

27. http://undertheblackflag.com – An interesting website covering Mediterranean piracy.

28. *Mameluke Sword*. http://en.wikipedia.org

29. http://www.globalsecurity.org/military/ops/barbary.htm - One of the best, if not the best, website on all things military.

30. http://www.earlyamerica.com/earlyamerica/milestones/whiskey - a good source on early American history with lots of primary historical references (e.g. contemporary newspaper articles).

31. http://en.wikipedia.org/penwar_e.htm

32. http://www.peninsularwar.org/penwar_e.htm

33. http://www.napoleon-series.org/research/government/Brazil/c_Independence.html

34. http://washington.org/visiting/experience~dc/knowledge_seeker/dc-history-african-american

35. http://www.aoc.gov/cc/capitol/capitol_construction.cfm

36. http://www.whitehouse.gov/about/presidents

37. http://en.wikipedia.org/wiki/War_of_1812

38. http://www.history.com/topics/war-of-1812

39. http://www.historycentral.com/1812/

Made in the USA
Lexington, KY
03 June 2012